— William Shakespeare's —
King Lear

adapted by **Brian Farrens**
illustrated by **Ben Dunn**

visit us at
www.abdopublishing.com

Published by Magic Wagon, a division of the ABDO Publishing Group, 8000 West 78th Street, Edina, Minnesota 55439. Copyright © 2009 by Abdo Consulting Group, Inc. International copyrights reserved in all countries. All rights reserved. No part of this book may be reproduced in any form without written permission from the publisher.
Graphic Planet™ is a trademark and logo of Magic Wagon.

Printed in the United States.

Adapted by Daniel Conner & Brian Farrens
Illustrated by Ben Dunn
Colored by Robby Bevard, Tony Galvan & Wes Hartman
Edited by Stephanie Hedlund and Rochelle Baltzer
Interior layout and design by Antarctic Press
Cover art by Ben Dunn
Cover design by Neil Klinepier

Library of Congress Cataloging-in-Publication Data

Farrens, Brian.
    William Shakespeare's King Lear / adapted by Brian Farrens; illustrated by Ben Dunn.
        p. cm. -- (Graphic Shakespeare)
    Summary: Shakespeare's tragedy of a royal father and his daughters is presented scene by scene in comic book format.
    ISBN 978-1-60270-189-2
    1. Graphic novels. [1. Graphic novels. 2. Shakespeare, William, 1564-1616--Adaptations.] I. Dunn, Ben, ill. II. Shakespeare, William, 1564-1616. King Lear. III. Title. IV. Title: King Lear.

PZ7.7.F37Wi 2008
741.5'973--dc22

                                                2008010739

Table of Contents

Cast of Characters...4

Our Setting...5

Act I...6

Act II...10

Act III..15

Act IV..25

Act V..34

Behind *King Lear*..44

Famous Phrases..45

About the Author..46

Additional Works by Shakespeare..........47

About the Adapter...47

Glossary...48

Web Sites...48

Cast of Characters

King Lear
King of Britain

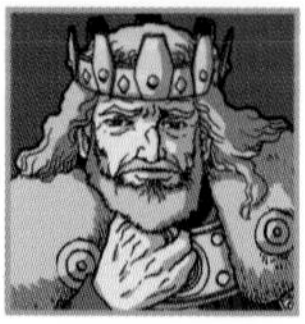

Goneril
Lear's eldest daughter

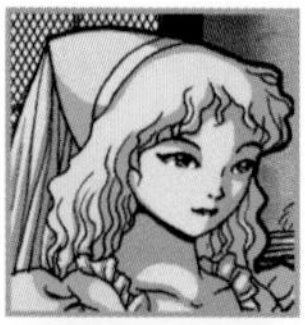

Regan
Lear's second-eldest daughter

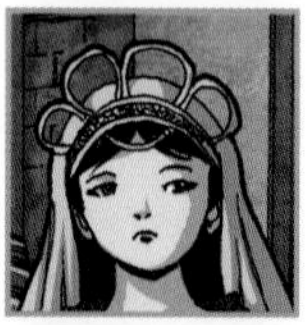

Cordelia
Lear's youngest daughter

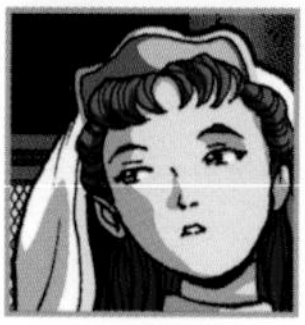

Albany
Duke of Albany, Goneril's husband

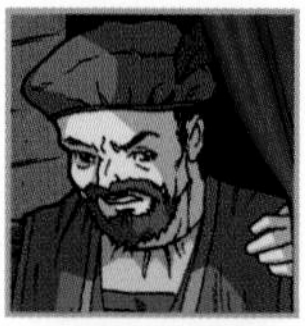

Cornwall
Duke of Cornwall, Regan's husband

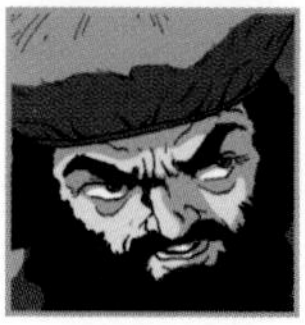

France
King of France, Cordelia's husband

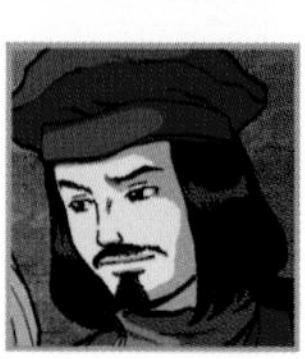

Gloucester
Father of Edgar and Edmund

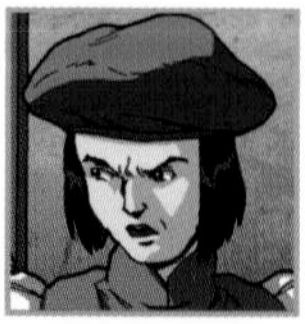

Edgar
Gloucester's legitimate son

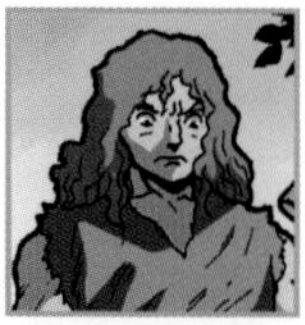

Edmund
Gloucester's illegitimate son

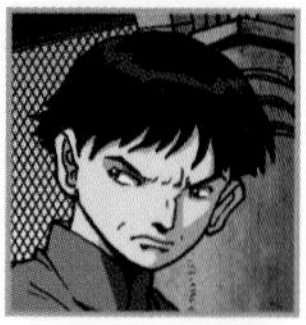

Kent
Earl of Kent

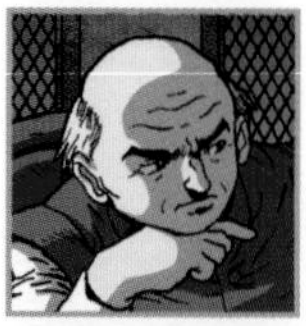

Fool
King Lear's court jester

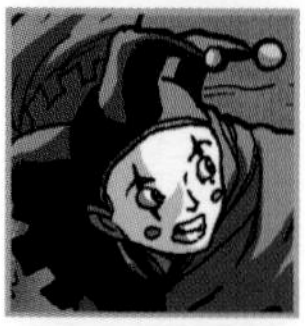

Oswald
Goneril's servant

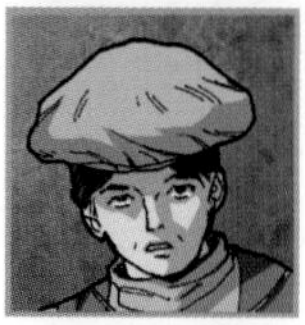

Gentleman
An attendant to Kent and Edgar

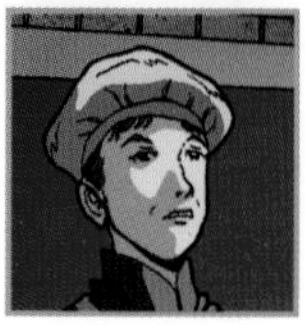

Our Setting

King Lear takes place in England on the islands of Great Britain before Christianity was established there. However, Shakespeare does not give exact locations for *King Lear*. Lear's palace or a battlefield are settings, but it does not say where these places are.

Little is known of the prehistoric era of England, but farming and weapons have been found dating back to 1200 BC. In 55 BC, Julius Caesar invaded Britain. For the next 20 years, Roman civilization spread throughout the area.

By AD 98, towns were established, including Gloucester and York. These towns are mentioned in Shakespeare's *King Lear*, though they are not noted as settings.

Roman and Celtic traditions were followed in England until Christianity arrived in 446. The traditions and government changed significantly after Christianity arrived.

Act I

King Lear gathers his daughters…

KNOW THAT WE HAVE DIVIDED IN THREE OUR KINGDOM, TO SHAKE ALL CARES AND BUSINESS FROM OUR AGE, CONFERRING THEM ON YOUNGER STRENGTHS WHILE WE UNBURDENED CRAWL TOWARD DEATH.

TELL ME, MY DAUGHTERS, WHICH OF YOU SHALL WE SAY DOTH LOVE US MOST?

SIR, I LOVE YOU MORE THAN WORD CAN WIELD THE MATTER.

IN MY TRUE HEART I FIND SHE NAMES MY VERY DEED OF LOVE; ONLY SHE COMES TOO SHORT. AND I FIND I AM ALONE FELICITATE IN YOUR DEAR HIGHNESS' LOVE.

NOW, OUR JOY, WHAT CAN YOU SAY TO DRAW A THIRD MORE OPULENT THAN YOUR SISTERS?

UNHAPPY THAT I AM, I CANNOT HEAVE MY HEART INTO MY MOUTH.

I LOVE YOUR MAJESTY ACCORDING TO MY BOND, NO MORE, NO LESS.

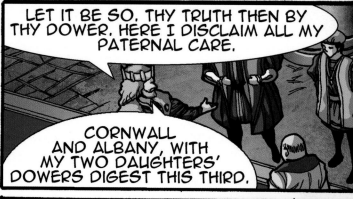

LET IT BE SO. THY TRUTH THEN BY THY DOWER. HERE I DISCLAIM ALL MY PATERNAL CARE.

CORNWALL AND ALBANY, WITH MY TWO DAUGHTERS' DOWERS DIGEST THIS THIRD.

Kent protests…

ROYAL LEAR, WHOM I HAVE EVER LOVED AS MY KING. THY YOUNGEST DAUGHTER DOES NOT LOVE THEE LEAST.

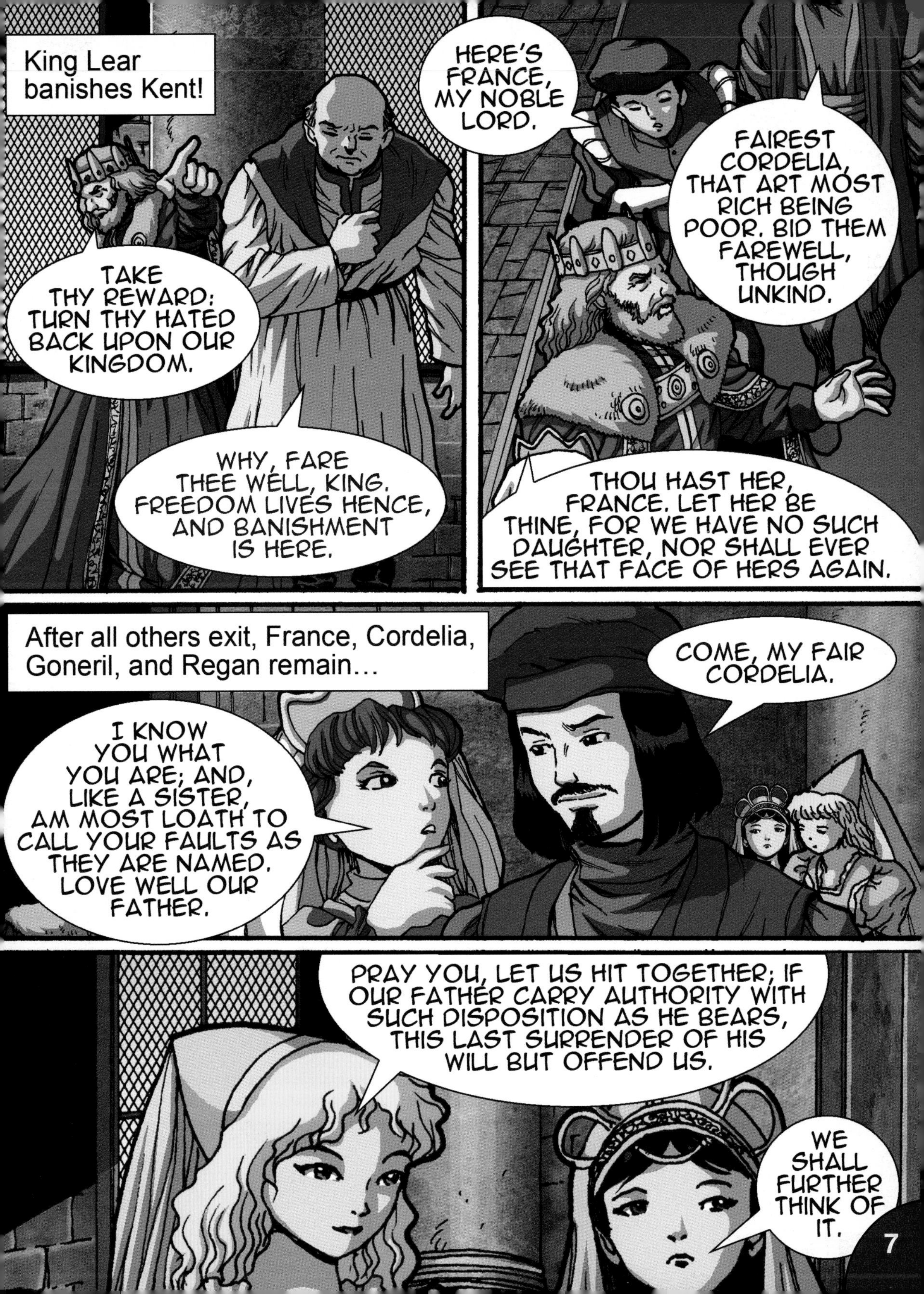

King Lear banishes Kent!
TAKE THY REWARD: TURN THY HATED BACK UPON OUR KINGDOM.
WHY, FARE THEE WELL, KING. FREEDOM LIVES HENCE, AND BANISHMENT IS HERE.
HERE'S FRANCE, MY NOBLE LORD.
FAIREST CORDELIA, THAT ART MOST RICH BEING POOR. BID THEM FAREWELL, THOUGH UNKIND.
THOU HAST HER, FRANCE. LET HER BE THINE, FOR WE HAVE NO SUCH DAUGHTER, NOR SHALL EVER SEE THAT FACE OF HERS AGAIN.
After all others exit, France, Cordelia, Goneril, and Regan remain…
COME, MY FAIR CORDELIA.
I KNOW YOU WHAT YOU ARE; AND, LIKE A SISTER, AM MOST LOATH TO CALL YOUR FAULTS AS THEY ARE NAMED. LOVE WELL OUR FATHER.
PRAY YOU, LET US HIT TOGETHER; IF OUR FATHER CARRY AUTHORITY WITH SUCH DISPOSITION AS HE BEARS, THIS LAST SURRENDER OF HIS WILL BUT OFFEND US.
WE SHALL FURTHER THINK OF IT.

At Gloucester's castle, Edmund has a letter...

Edmund's father, Gloucester, enters…

WHY SO EARNESTLY SEEK YOU TO PUT UP THAT LETTER?

IT IS A LETTER FROM MY BROTHER THAT I HAVE NOT ALL O'ERREAD.

GIVE ME THE LETTER, SIR.

HUM! CONSPIRACY? 'SLEEP TILL I WAKED HIM, YOU SHOULD ENJOY HALF HIS REVENUE.' MY SON EDGAR! HE CANNOT BE SUCH A MONSTER.

NOR IS NOT, SURE.

WHEREFORE SHOULD STAND IN THE PLAGUE OF CUSTOM TO DEPRIVE ME FOR THAT I AM SOME TWELVE OR FOURTEEN MOONSHINES LAG OF A BROTHER?

FIND OUT THIS VILLAIN, EDMUND; IT SHALL LOSE THEE NOTHING.

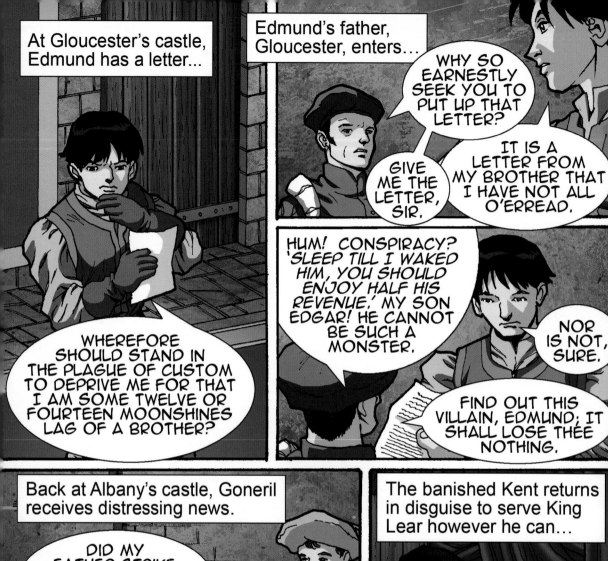

Back at Albany's castle, Goneril receives distressing news.

The banished Kent returns in disguise to serve King Lear however he can…

DID MY FATHER STRIKE MY GENTLEMAN FOR CHIDING OF HIS FOOL?

AY MADAM.

BY DAY AND NIGHT HE WRONGS ME. HIS KNIGHTS GROW RIOTOUS, AND HIMSELF UPBRAIDS US ON EVERY TRIFLE. I WILL NOT SPEAK WITH HIM.

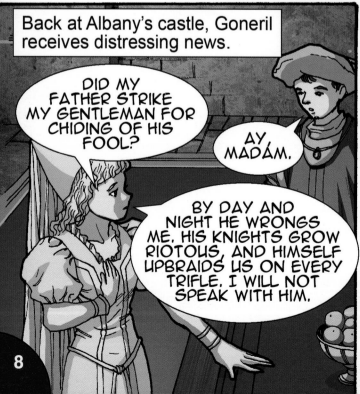

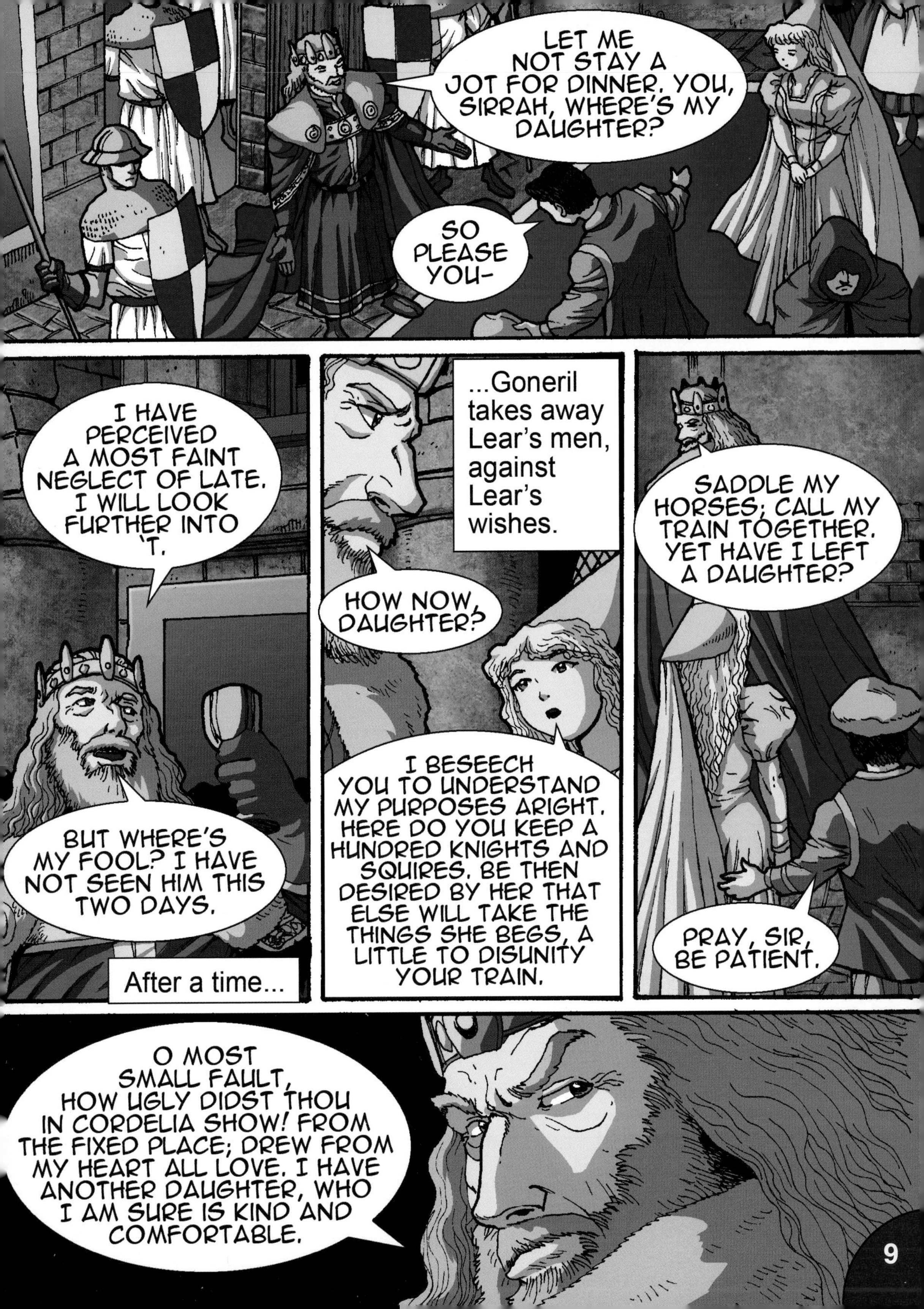

LET ME NOT STAY A JOT FOR DINNER. YOU, SIRRAH, WHERE'S MY DAUGHTER?
SO PLEASE YOU-
I HAVE PERCEIVED A MOST FAINT NEGLECT OF LATE. I WILL LOOK FURTHER INTO 'T.
BUT WHERE'S MY FOOL? I HAVE NOT SEEN HIM THIS TWO DAYS.
After a time...
...Goneril takes away Lear's men, against Lear's wishes.
HOW NOW, DAUGHTER?
I BESEECH YOU TO UNDERSTAND MY PURPOSES ARIGHT. HERE DO YOU KEEP A HUNDRED KNIGHTS AND SQUIRES. BE THEN DESIRED BY HER THAT ELSE WILL TAKE THE THINGS SHE BEGS, A LITTLE TO DISUNITY YOUR TRAIN.
SADDLE MY HORSES; CALL MY TRAIN TOGETHER. YET HAVE I LEFT A DAUGHTER?
PRAY, SIR, BE PATIENT.
O MOST SMALL FAULT, HOW UGLY DIDST THOU IN CORDELIA SHOW! FROM THE FIXED PLACE; DREW FROM MY HEART ALL LOVE. I HAVE ANOTHER DAUGHTER, WHO I AM SURE IS KIND AND COMFORTABLE.

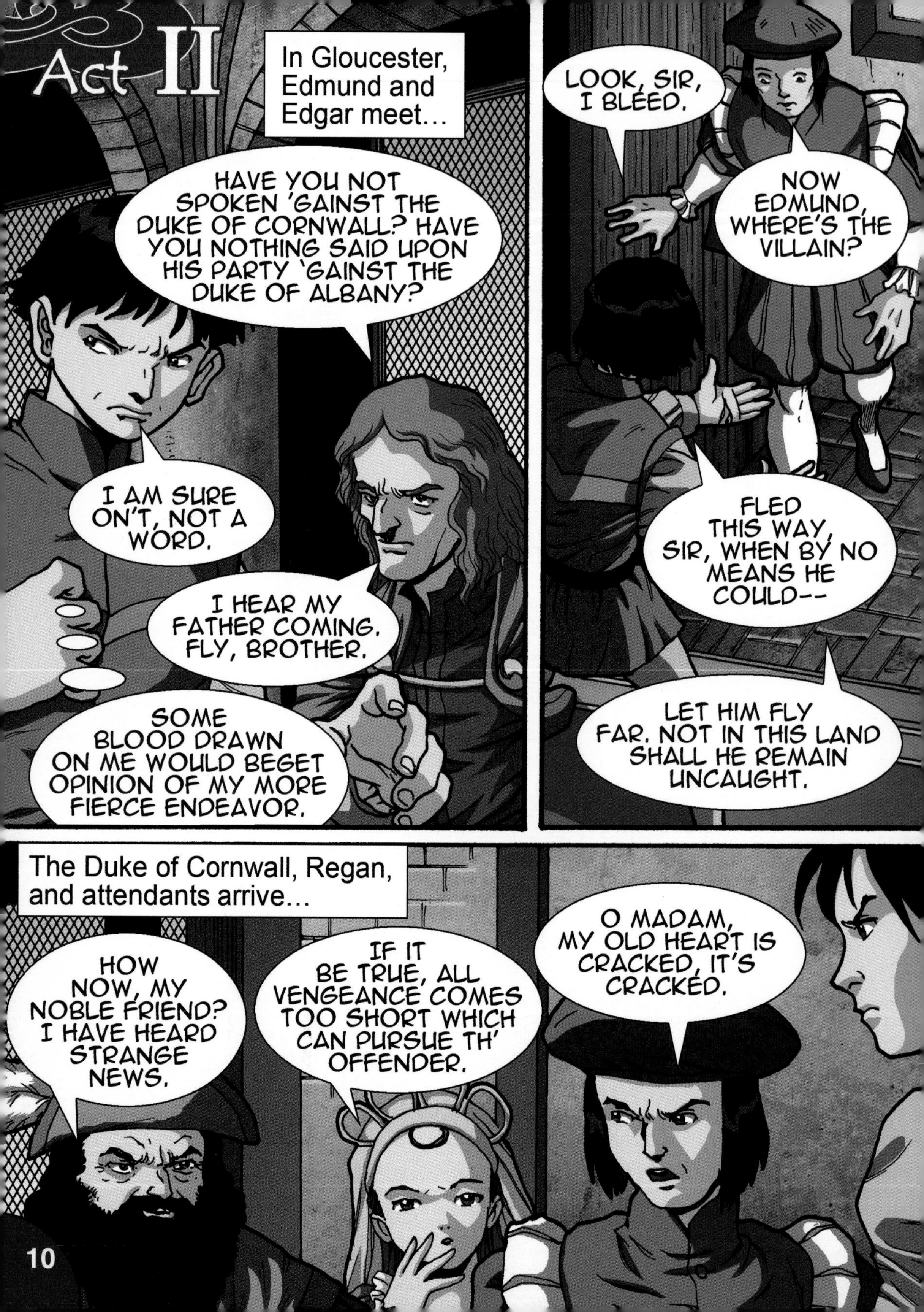
Act II
In Gloucester, Edmund and Edgar meet…
HAVE YOU NOT SPOKEN 'GAINST THE DUKE OF CORNWALL? HAVE YOU NOTHING SAID UPON HIS PARTY 'GAINST THE DUKE OF ALBANY?
I AM SURE ON'T, NOT A WORD.
I HEAR MY FATHER COMING. FLY, BROTHER.
SOME BLOOD DRAWN ON ME WOULD BEGET OPINION OF MY MORE FIERCE ENDEAVOR.
LOOK, SIR, I BLEED.
NOW EDMUND, WHERE'S THE VILLAIN?
FLED THIS WAY, SIR, WHEN BY NO MEANS HE COULD--
LET HIM FLY FAR. NOT IN THIS LAND SHALL HE REMAIN UNCAUGHT.
The Duke of Cornwall, Regan, and attendants arrive…
HOW NOW, MY NOBLE FRIEND? I HAVE HEARD STRANGE NEWS.
IF IT BE TRUE, ALL VENGEANCE COMES TOO SHORT WHICH CAN PURSUE TH' OFFENDER.
O MADAM, MY OLD HEART IS CRACKED, IT'S CRACKED.

In another part of the city, Kent and Oswald trade insults.

HOW NOW? WHAT'S THE MATTER?

WEAPONS, ARMS? WHAT'S THE MATTER HERE?

FELLOW, I KNOW THEE. THOU ART NOTHING BUT THE COMPOSITION OF A KNAVE, BEGGAR, COWARD. ONE WHOM I WILL BEAT INTO CLAMOROUS WHINING IF THOU DENY'ST.

WHY, WHAT A MONSTROUS FELLOW ART THOU!

THAT SUCH A SLAVE AS THIS SHOULD WEAR A SWORD, WHO WEARS NO HONESTY.

FETCH FORTH THE STOCKS!

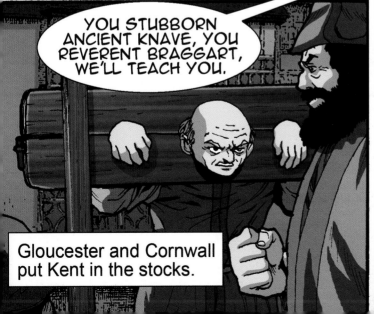

YOU STUBBORN ANCIENT KNAVE, YOU REVERENT BRAGGART, WE'LL TEACH YOU.

Gloucester and Cornwall put Kent in the stocks.

ALL WEARY AND O'ERWATCHED, TAKE VANTAGE, HEAVY EYES, NOT TO BEHOLD THIS SHAMEFUL LODGING.

11

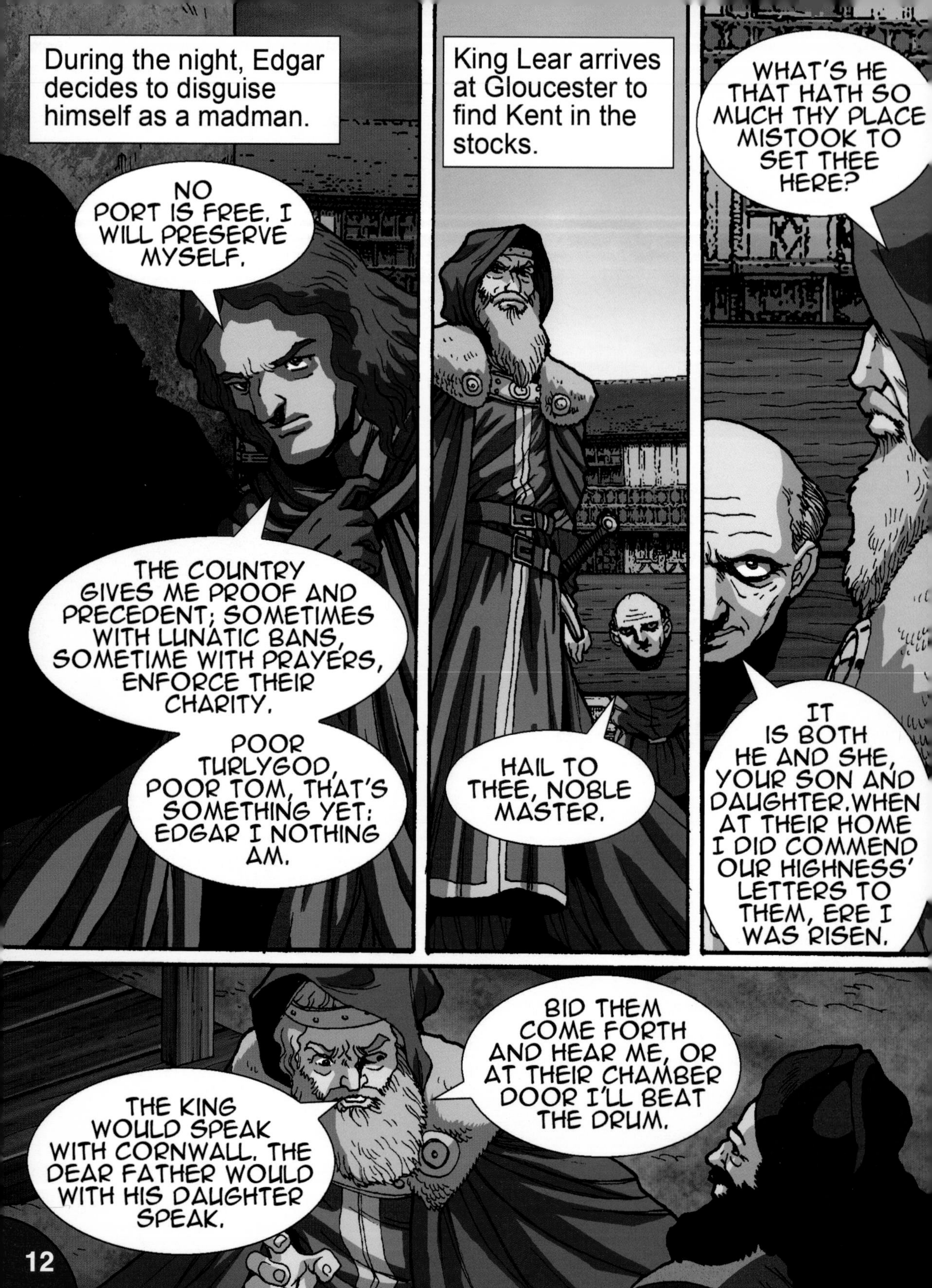
During the night, Edgar decides to disguise himself as a madman.
NO PORT IS FREE. I WILL PRESERVE MYSELF.
THE COUNTRY GIVES ME PROOF AND PRECEDENT; SOMETIMES WITH LUNATIC BANS, SOMETIME WITH PRAYERS, ENFORCE THEIR CHARITY.
POOR TURLYGOD, POOR TOM, THAT'S SOMETHING YET: EDGAR I NOTHING AM.
King Lear arrives at Gloucester to find Kent in the stocks.
HAIL TO THEE, NOBLE MASTER.
WHAT'S HE THAT HATH SO MUCH THY PLACE MISTOOK TO SET THEE HERE?
IT IS BOTH HE AND SHE, YOUR SON AND DAUGHTER. WHEN AT THEIR HOME I DID COMMEND OUR HIGHNESS' LETTERS TO THEM, ERE I WAS RISEN.
THE KING WOULD SPEAK WITH CORNWALL. THE DEAR FATHER WOULD WITH HIS DAUGHTER SPEAK.
BID THEM COME FORTH AND HEAR ME, OR AT THEIR CHAMBER DOOR I'LL BEAT THE DRUM.

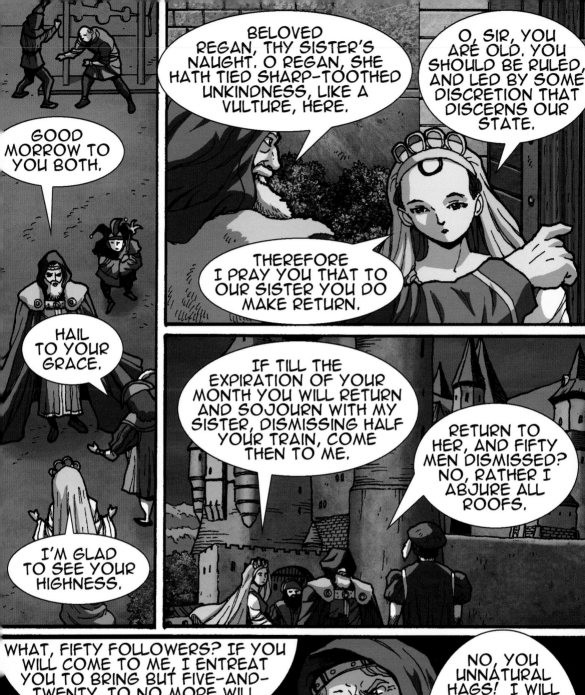

GOOD MORROW TO YOU BOTH.

BELOVED REGAN, THY SISTER'S NAUGHT. O REGAN, SHE HATH TIED SHARP-TOOTHED UNKINDNESS, LIKE A VULTURE, HERE.

O, SIR, YOU ARE OLD. YOU SHOULD BE RULED, AND LED BY SOME DISCRETION THAT DISCERNS OUR STATE.

THEREFORE I PRAY YOU THAT TO OUR SISTER YOU DO MAKE RETURN.

HAIL TO YOUR GRACE.

I'M GLAD TO SEE YOUR HIGHNESS.

IF TILL THE EXPIRATION OF YOUR MONTH YOU WILL RETURN AND SOJOURN WITH MY SISTER, DISMISSING HALF YOUR TRAIN, COME THEN TO ME.

RETURN TO HER, AND FIFTY MEN DISMISSED? NO, RATHER I ABJURE ALL ROOFS.

WHAT, FIFTY FOLLOWERS? IF YOU WILL COME TO ME, I ENTREAT YOU TO BRING BUT FIVE-AND-TWENTY. TO NO MORE WILL I GIVE PLACE OR NOTICE.

NO, YOU UNNATURAL HAGS! I WILL HAVE SUCH REVENGES ON YOU BOTH WHAT THEY ARE, YET I KNOW NOT; BUT THEY SHALL BE THE TERRORS OF THE EARTH.

13

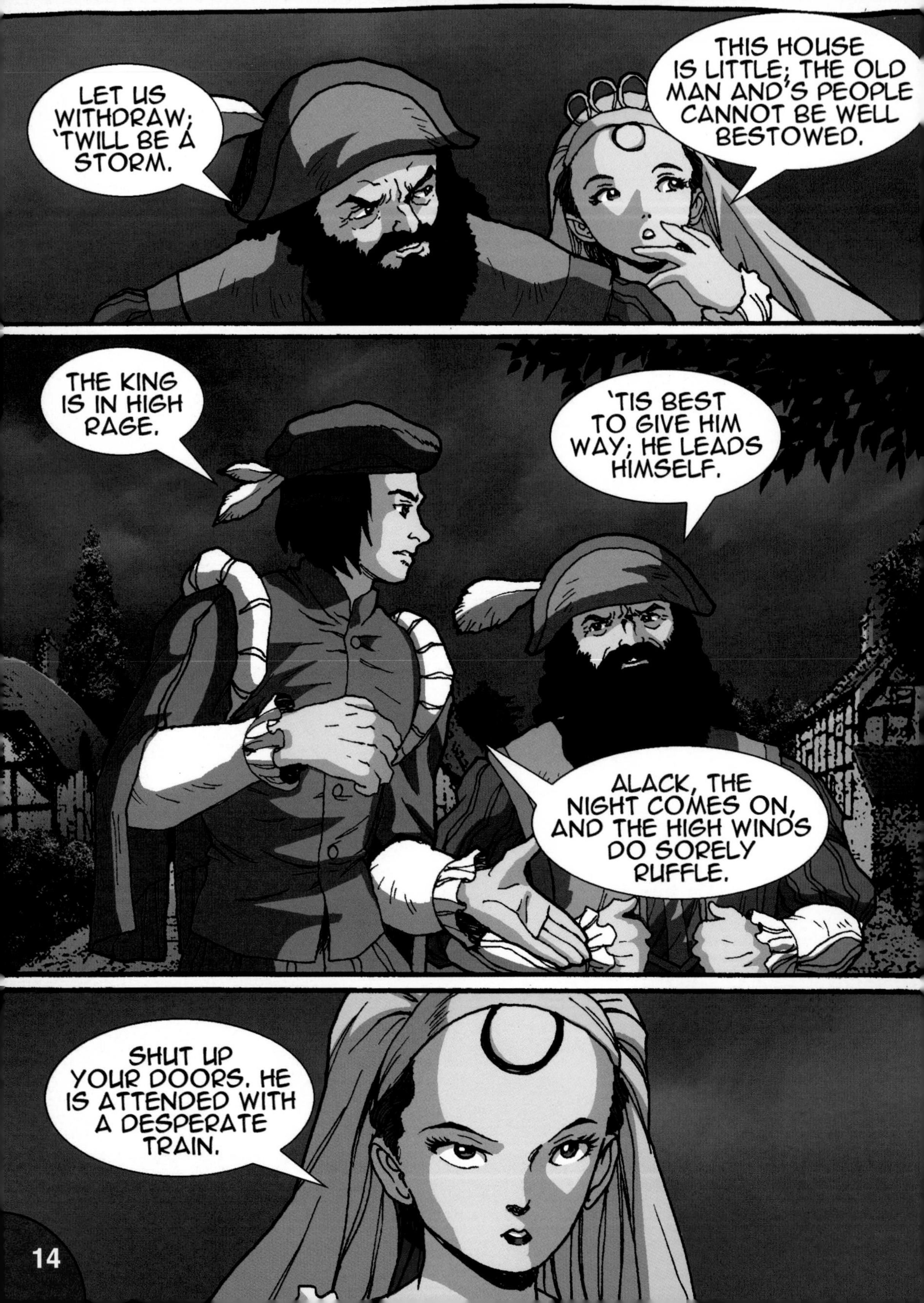
LET US WITHDRAW; 'TWILL BE A STORM.
THIS HOUSE IS LITTLE; THE OLD MAN AND'S PEOPLE CANNOT BE WELL BESTOWED.
THE KING IS IN HIGH RAGE.
'TIS BEST TO GIVE HIM WAY; HE LEADS HIMSELF.
ALACK, THE NIGHT COMES ON, AND THE HIGH WINDS DO SORELY RUFFLE.
SHUT UP YOUR DOORS. HE IS ATTENDED WITH A DESPERATE TRAIN.

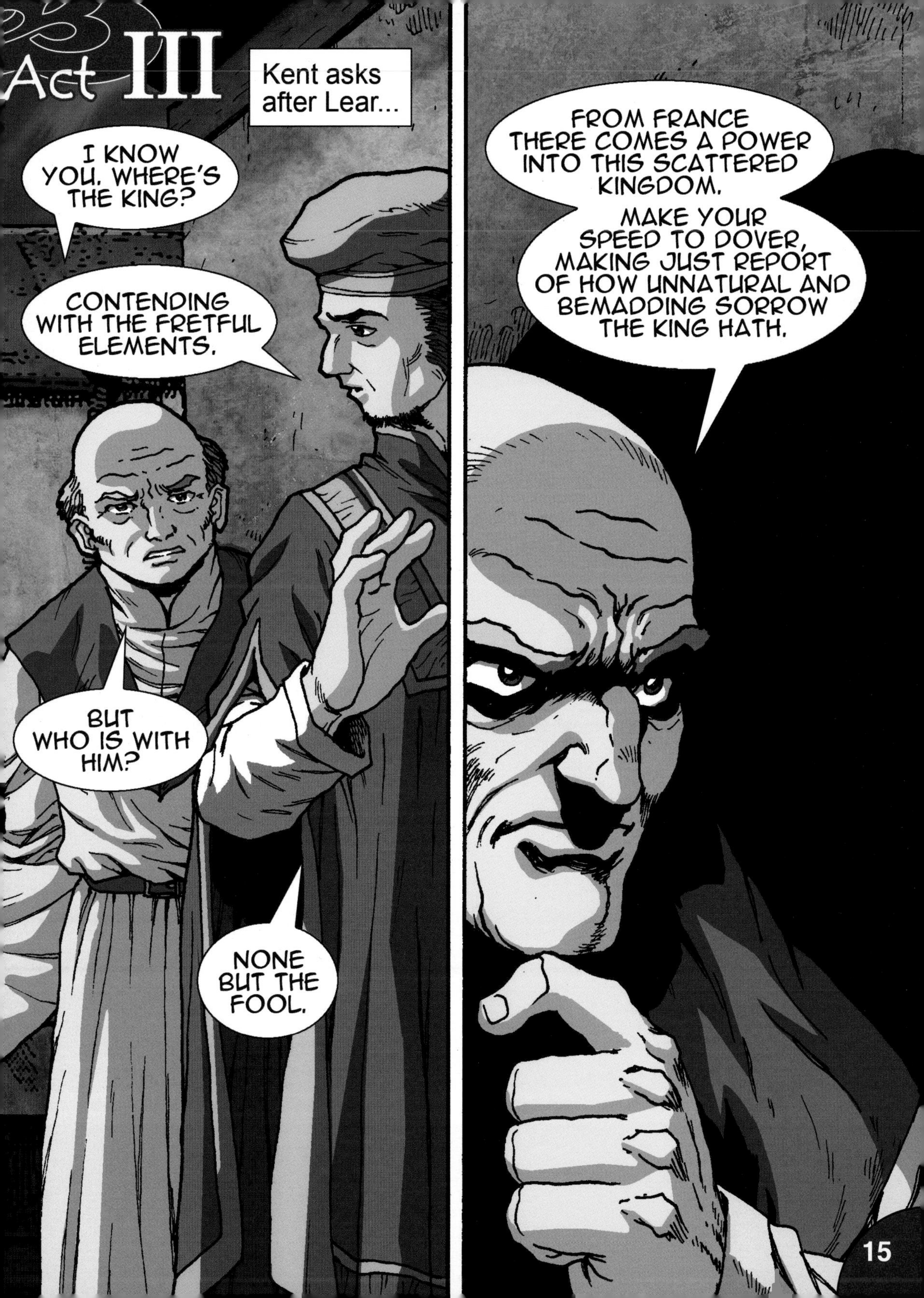

Act III
Kent asks after Lear...
I KNOW YOU. WHERE'S THE KING?
CONTENDING WITH THE FRETFUL ELEMENTS.
BUT WHO IS WITH HIM?
NONE BUT THE FOOL.
FROM FRANCE THERE COMES A POWER INTO THIS SCATTERED KINGDOM.
MAKE YOUR SPEED TO DOVER, MAKING JUST REPORT OF HOW UNNATURAL AND BEMADDING SORROW THE KING HATH.

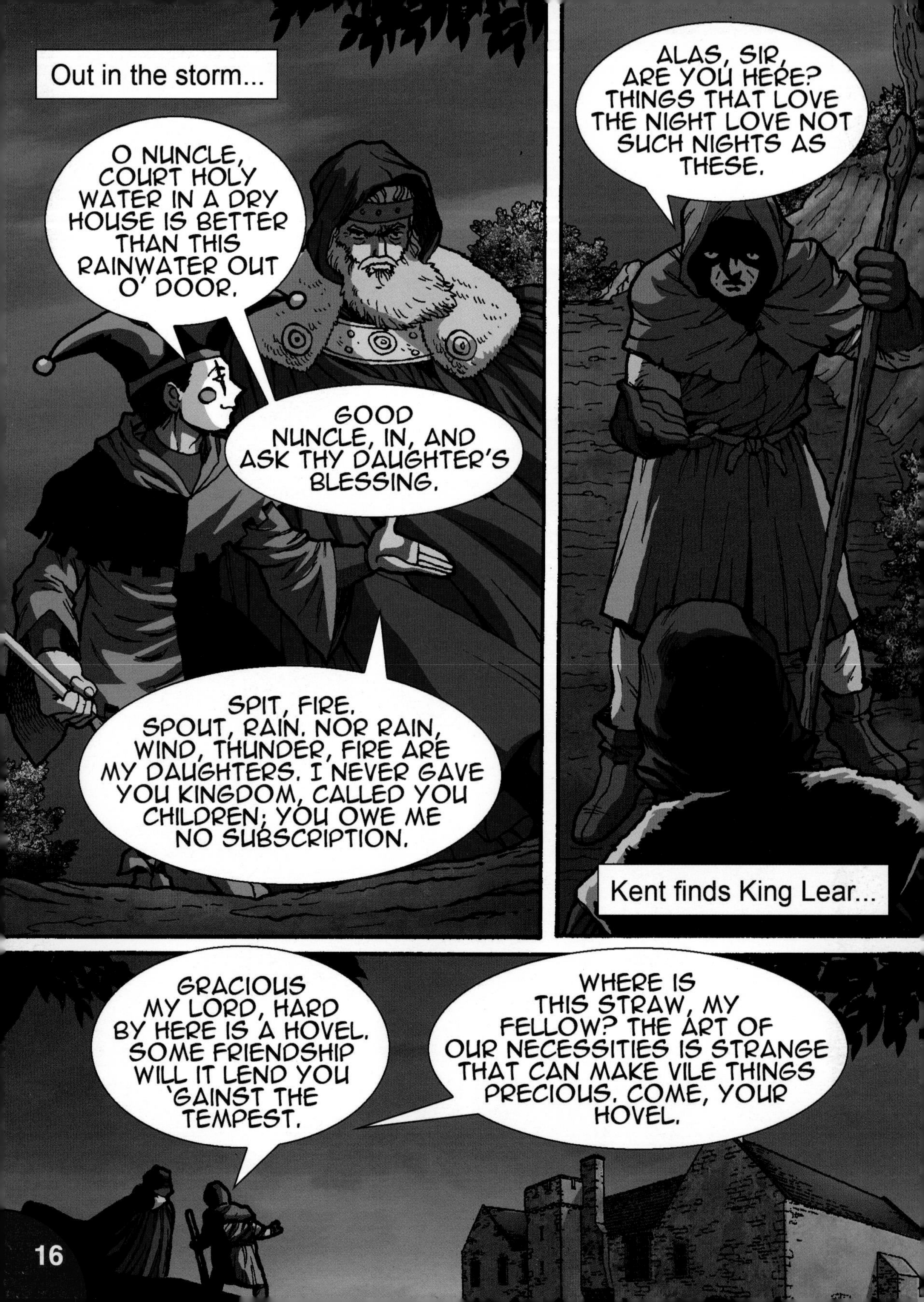

Out in the storm...
O NUNCLE, COURT HOLY WATER IN A DRY HOUSE IS BETTER THAN THIS RAINWATER OUT O' DOOR.
GOOD NUNCLE, IN, AND ASK THY DAUGHTER'S BLESSING.
SPIT, FIRE. SPOUT, RAIN. NOR RAIN, WIND, THUNDER, FIRE ARE MY DAUGHTERS. I NEVER GAVE YOU KINGDOM, CALLED YOU CHILDREN; YOU OWE ME NO SUBSCRIPTION.
ALAS, SIR, ARE YOU HERE? THINGS THAT LOVE THE NIGHT LOVE NOT SUCH NIGHTS AS THESE.
Kent finds King Lear...
GRACIOUS MY LORD, HARD BY HERE IS A HOVEL. SOME FRIENDSHIP WILL IT LEND YOU 'GAINST THE TEMPEST.
WHERE IS THIS STRAW, MY FELLOW? THE ART OF OUR NECESSITIES IS STRANGE THAT CAN MAKE VILE THINGS PRECIOUS. COME, YOUR HOVEL.

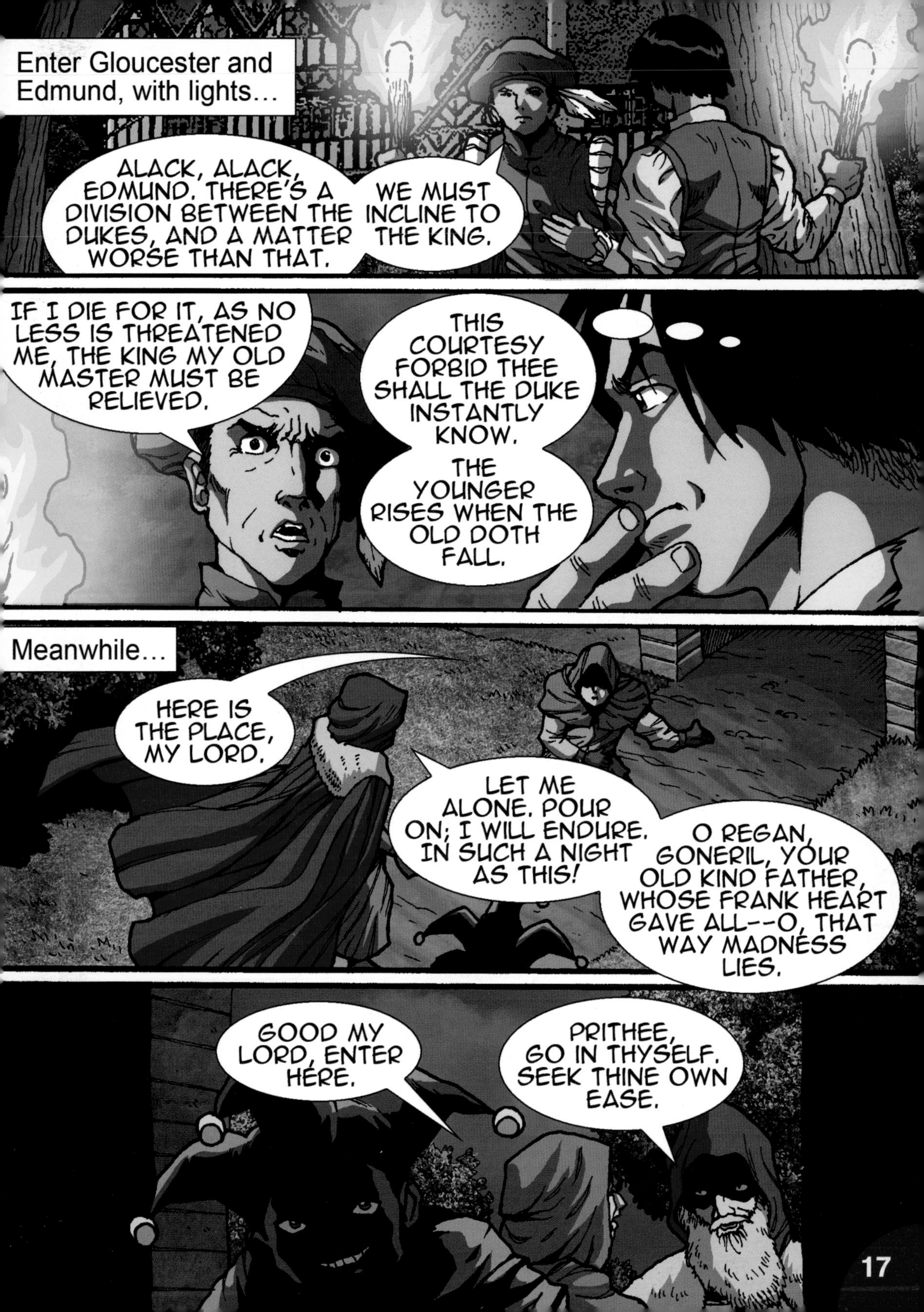
Enter Gloucester and Edmund, with lights…
ALACK, ALACK, EDMUND. THERE'S A DIVISION BETWEEN THE DUKES, AND A MATTER WORSE THAN THAT.
WE MUST INCLINE TO THE KING.
IF I DIE FOR IT, AS NO LESS IS THREATENED ME, THE KING MY OLD MASTER MUST BE RELIEVED.
THIS COURTESY FORBID THEE SHALL THE DUKE INSTANTLY KNOW.
THE YOUNGER RISES WHEN THE OLD DOTH FALL.
Meanwhile…
HERE IS THE PLACE, MY LORD.
LET ME ALONE. POUR ON; I WILL ENDURE. IN SUCH A NIGHT AS THIS!
O REGAN, GONERIL, YOUR OLD KIND FATHER, WHOSE FRANK HEART GAVE ALL--O, THAT WAY MADNESS LIES.
GOOD MY LORD, ENTER HERE.
PRITHEE, GO IN THYSELF. SEEK THINE OWN EASE.

COME NOT IN HERE, NUNCLE; HERE'S A SPIRIT. HELP ME, HELP ME!

AWAY! THE FOUL FIEND FOLLOWS ME! GO TO THY COLD BED AND WARM THEE.

O, DO, DE, DO, DE DO, DE. DO POOR TOM SOME CHARITY.

HAS HIS DAUGHTERS BROUGHT HIM TO THIS PASS?

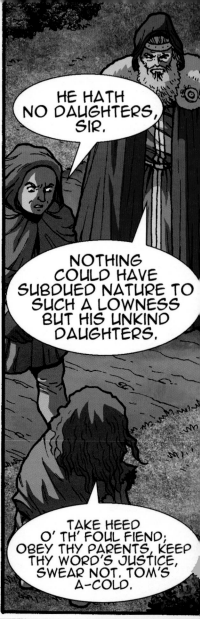

HE HATH NO DAUGHTERS, SIR.

NOTHING COULD HAVE SUBDUED NATURE TO SUCH A LOWNESS BUT HIS UNKIND DAUGHTERS.

TAKE HEED O' TH' FOUL FIEND; OBEY THY PARENTS, KEEP THY WORD'S JUSTICE, SWEAR NOT. TOM'S A-COLD.

Enter Gloucester with a torch…

OUR FLESH AND BLOOD, MY LORD, IS GROWN SO VILE THAT IT DOTH HATE WHAT GETS IT. YET HAVE I VENTURED TO COME SEEK YOU OUT AND BRING YOU WHERE BOTH FIRE AND FOOD IS READY.

FIRST LET ME TALK WITH THIS PHILOSOPHER.

18

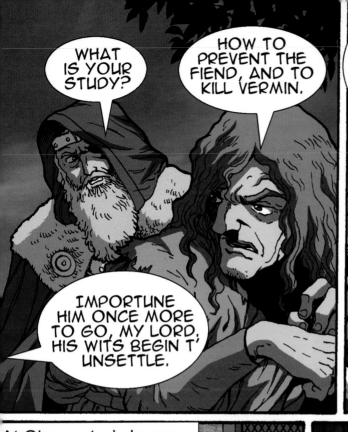

WHAT IS YOUR STUDY?

HOW TO PREVENT THE FIEND, AND TO KILL VERMIN.

IMPORTUNE HIM ONCE MORE TO GO, MY LORD; HIS WITS BEGIN T' UNSETTLE.

CANST THOU BLAME HIM? HIS DAUGHTERS SEEK HIS DEATH. I AM ALMOST MAD MYSELF. I HAD A SON; HE SOUGHT MY LIFE. THE GRIEF HATH CRAZED MY WITS. WHAT A NIGHT'S THIS!

COME LET'S IN ALL.

At Gloucester's home...

I WILL HAVE MY REVENGE ERE I DEPART HIS HOUSE.

THIS IS THE LETTER WHICH HE SPOKE OF...

...WHICH APPROVES HIM AN INTELLIGENT PARTY TO THE ADVANTAGES OF FRANCE.

TRUE OR FALSE, IT HATH MADE THEE EARL OF GLOUCESTER. SEEK OUT WHERE THY FATHER IS.

IF I FIND HIM COMFORTING THE KING, IT WILL STUFF HIS SUSPICION MORE FULLY.

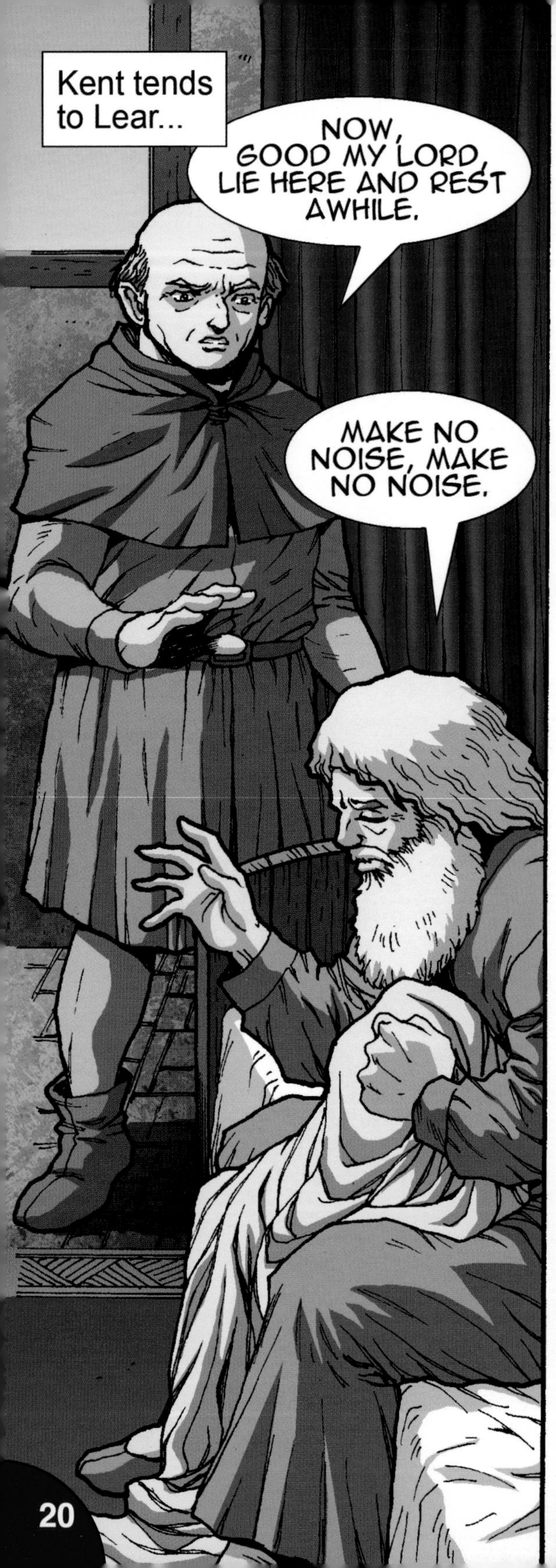
Kent tends to Lear...
NOW, GOOD MY LORD, LIE HERE AND REST AWHILE.
MAKE NO NOISE, MAKE NO NOISE.

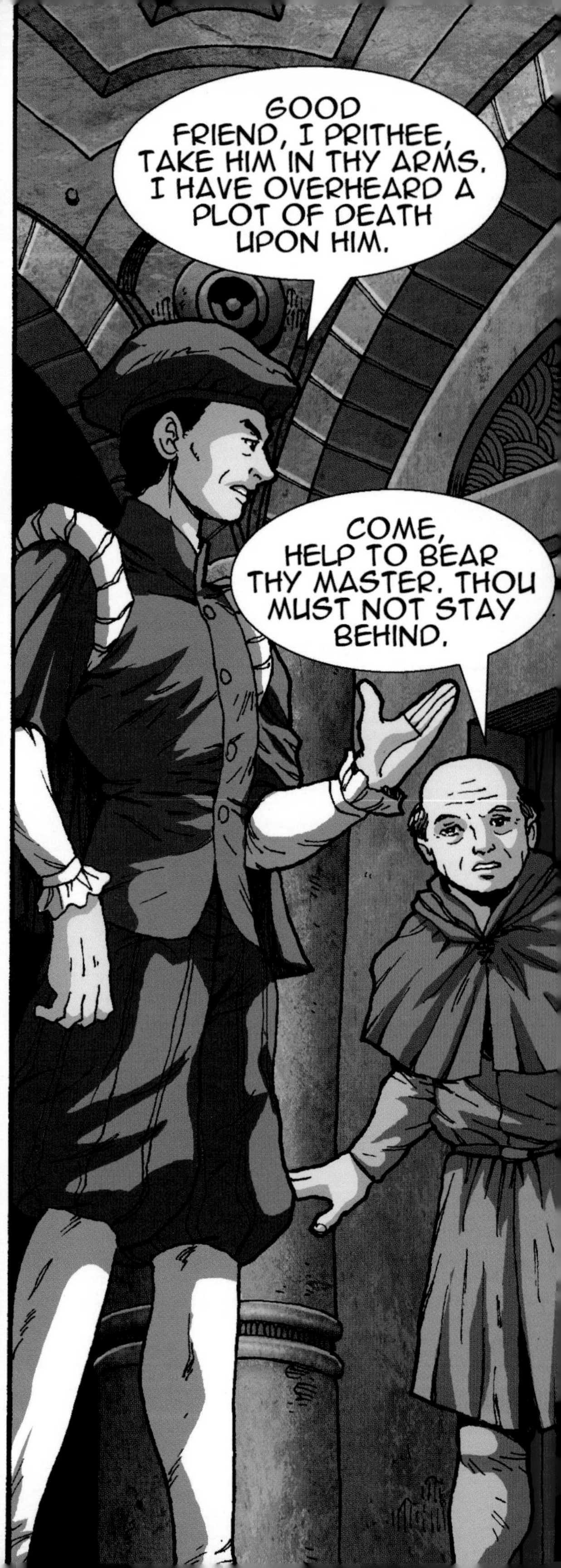
GOOD FRIEND, I PRITHEE, TAKE HIM IN THY ARMS. I HAVE OVERHEARD A PLOT OF DEATH UPON HIM.
COME, HELP TO BEAR THY MASTER. THOU MUST NOT STAY BEHIND.

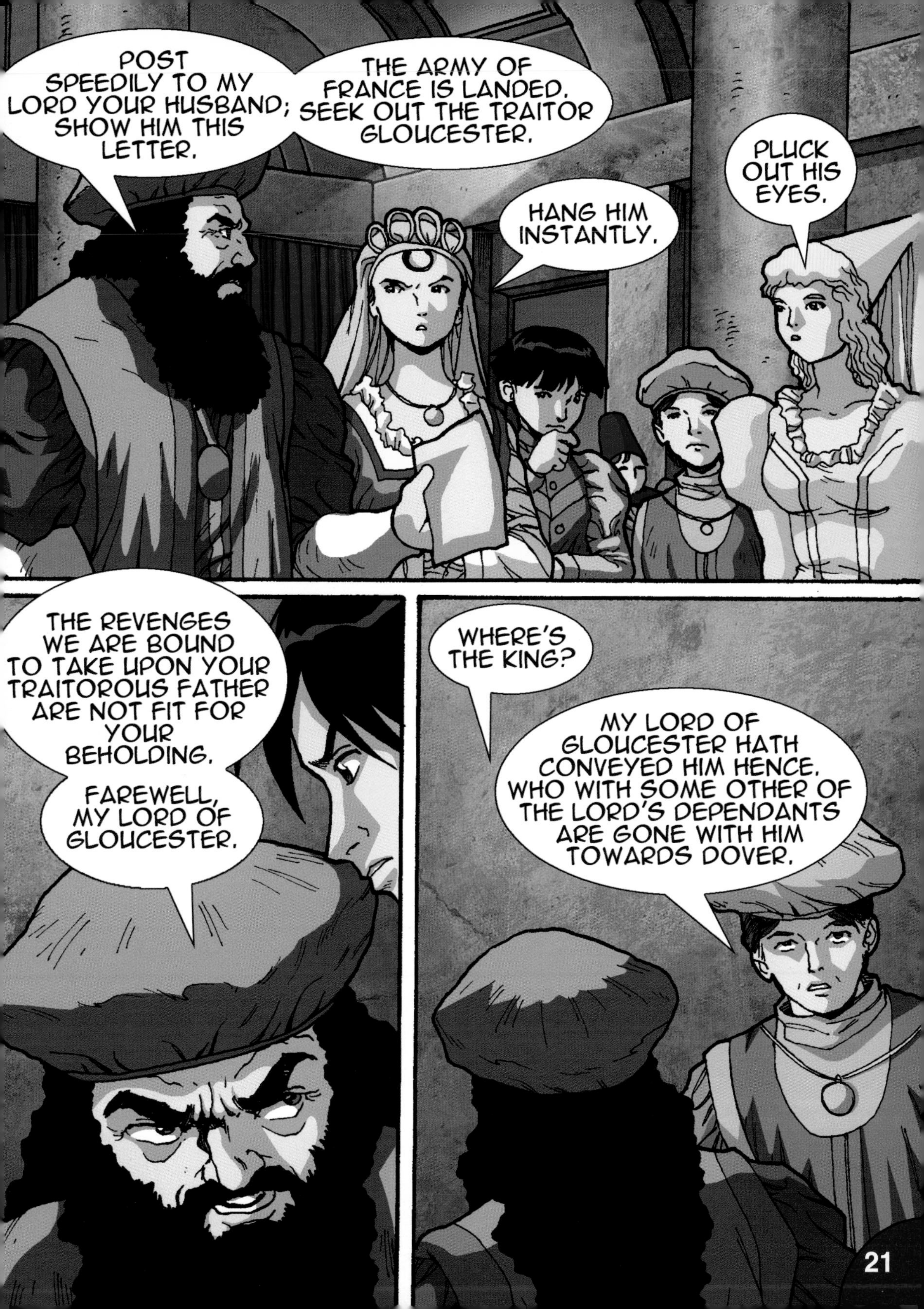
POST SPEEDILY TO MY LORD YOUR HUSBAND; SHOW HIM THIS LETTER.
THE ARMY OF FRANCE IS LANDED. SEEK OUT THE TRAITOR GLOUCESTER.
HANG HIM INSTANTLY.
PLUCK OUT HIS EYES.
THE REVENGES WE ARE BOUND TO TAKE UPON YOUR TRAITOROUS FATHER ARE NOT FIT FOR YOUR BEHOLDING.
FAREWELL, MY LORD OF GLOUCESTER.
WHERE'S THE KING?
MY LORD OF GLOUCESTER HATH CONVEYED HIM HENCE. WHO WITH SOME OTHER OF THE LORD'S DEPENDANTS ARE GONE WITH HIM TOWARDS DOVER.

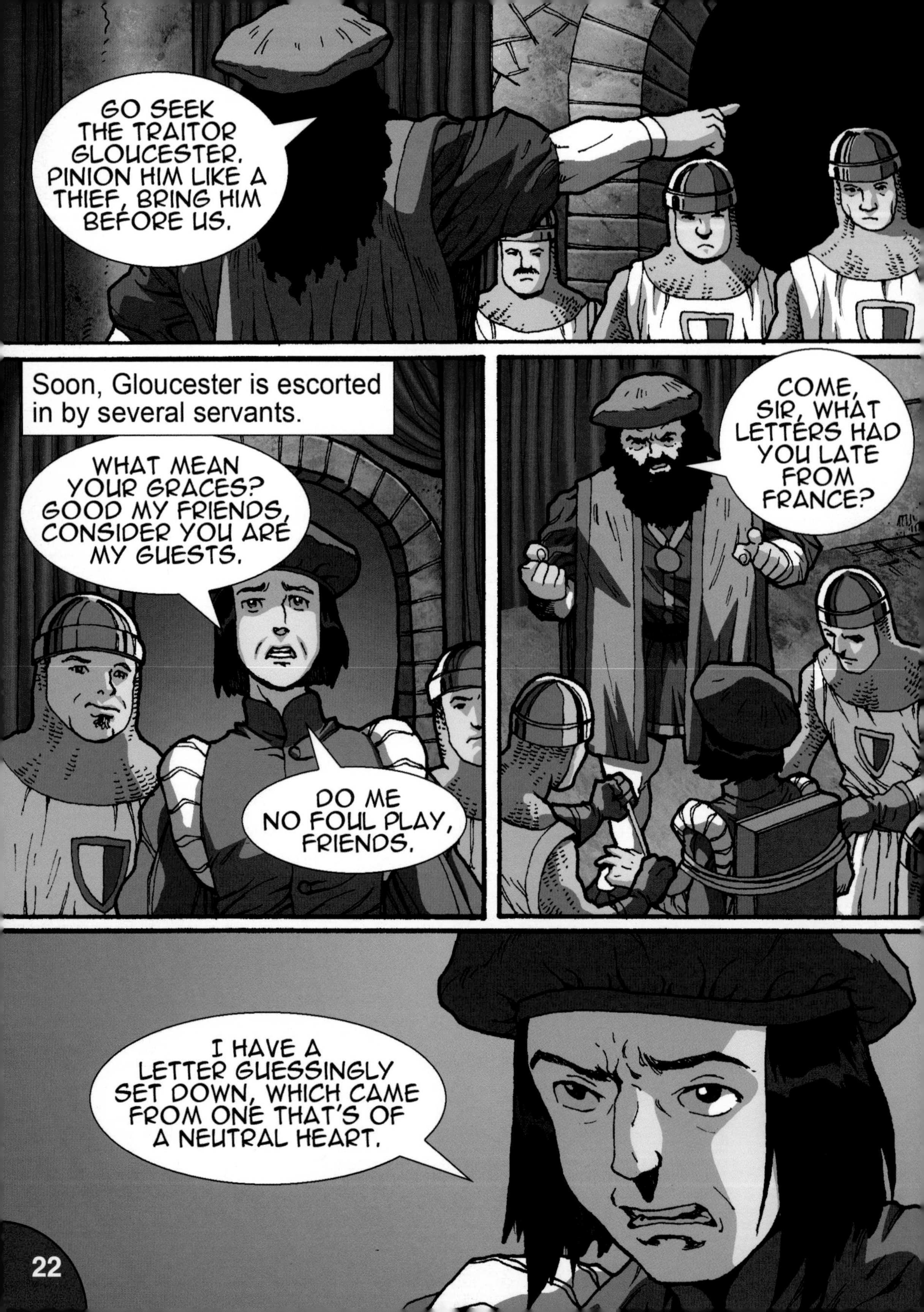
GO SEEK THE TRAITOR GLOUCESTER. PINION HIM LIKE A THIEF, BRING HIM BEFORE US.
Soon, Gloucester is escorted in by several servants.
WHAT MEAN YOUR GRACES? GOOD MY FRIENDS, CONSIDER YOU ARE MY GUESTS.
DO ME NO FOUL PLAY, FRIENDS.
COME, SIR, WHAT LETTERS HAD YOU LATE FROM FRANCE?
I HAVE A LETTER GUESSINGLY SET DOWN, WHICH CAME FROM ONE THAT'S OF A NEUTRAL HEART.

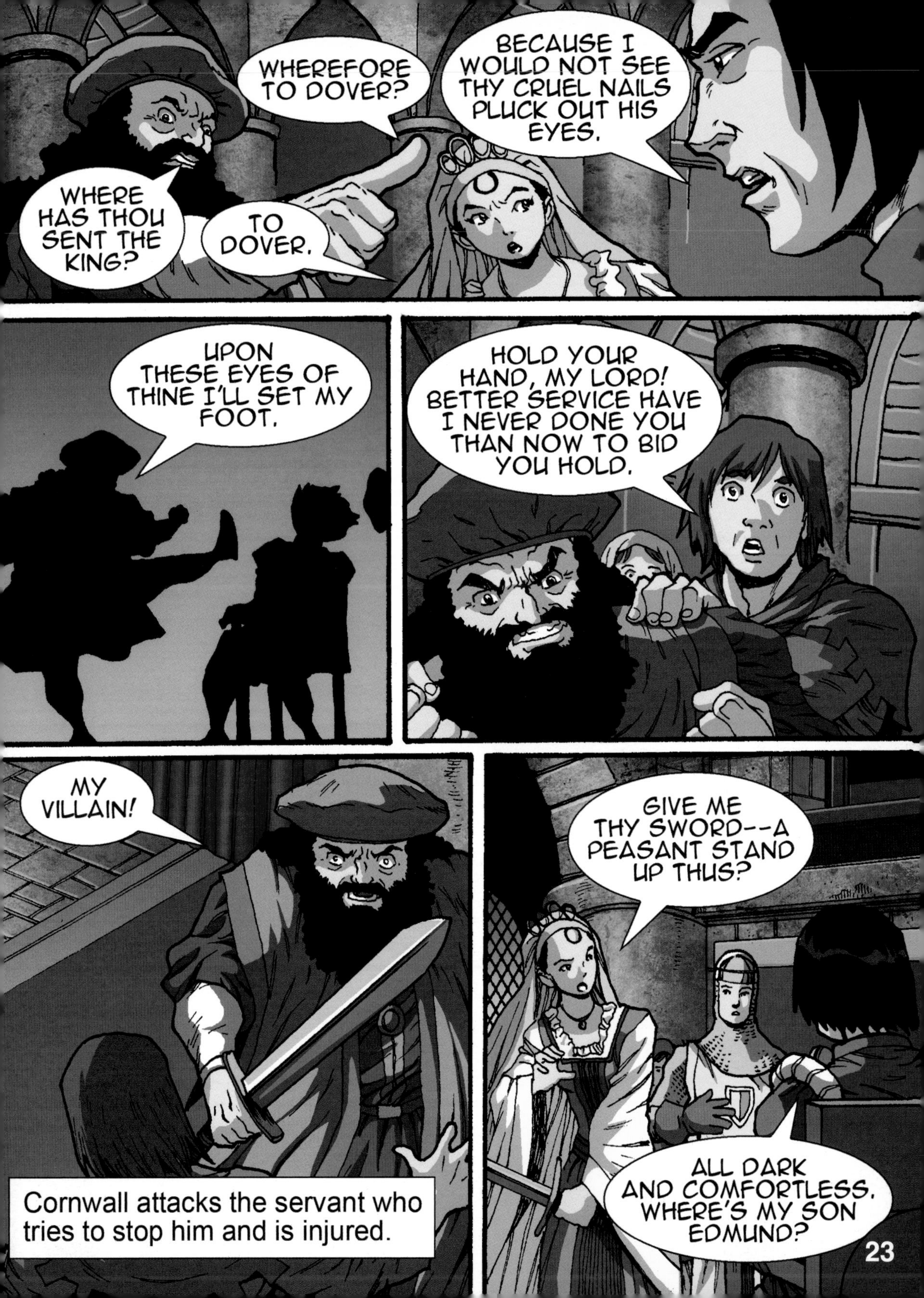
WHERE HAS THOU SENT THE KING?
TO DOVER.
WHEREFORE TO DOVER?
BECAUSE I WOULD NOT SEE THY CRUEL NAILS PLUCK OUT HIS EYES.
UPON THESE EYES OF THINE I'LL SET MY FOOT.
HOLD YOUR HAND, MY LORD! BETTER SERVICE HAVE I NEVER DONE YOU THAN NOW TO BID YOU HOLD.
MY VILLAIN!
Cornwall attacks the servant who tries to stop him and is injured.
GIVE ME THY SWORD--A PEASANT STAND UP THUS?
ALL DARK AND COMFORTLESS. WHERE'S MY SON EDMUND?

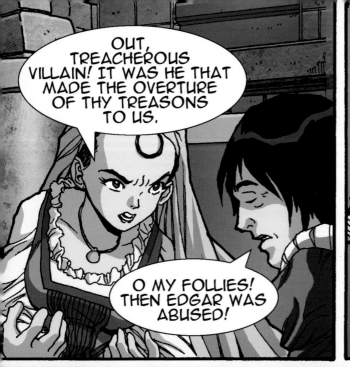

OUT, TREACHEROUS VILLAIN! IT WAS HE THAT MADE THE OVERTURE OF THY TREASONS TO US.

O MY FOLLIES! THEN EDGAR WAS ABUSED!

GO THRUST HIM OUT AT GATES, AND LET HIM SMELL HIS WAY TO DOVER.

I HAVE A HURT. TURN OUT THAT EYELESS VILLAIN. REGAN, I BLEED APACE.

IF SHE LIVE LONG, AND IN THE END MEET THE OLD COURSE OF DEATH, WOMEN WILL ALL TURN MONSTERS.

LET'S FOLLOW THE OLD EARL, AND GET THE BEDLAM TO LEAD HIM WHERE HE WOULD.

Act IV

On the road to Dover…

BUT WHO COMES HERE? MY FATHER, POORLY LED?

YOU CANNOT SEE YOUR WAY.

I STUMBLED WHEN I SAW.

O DEAR SON EDGAR, MIGHT I BUT LIVE TO SEE THEE IN MY TOUCH. HOW NOW? WHO'S THERE?

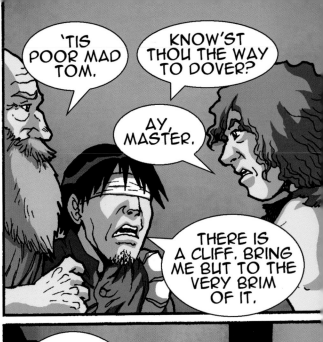

'TIS POOR MAD TOM.

KNOW'ST THOU THE WAY TO DOVER?

AY, MASTER.

THERE IS A CLIFF. BRING ME BUT TO THE VERY BRIM OF IT.

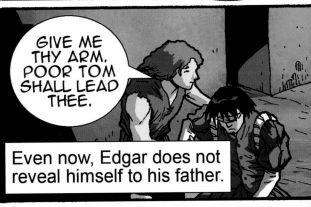

GIVE ME THY ARM, POOR TOM SHALL LEAD THEE.

Even now, Edgar does not reveal himself to his father.

Soon, Goneril arrives at Albany's castle.

NOW, WHERE'S YOUR MASTER?

MADAM, WITHIN. I TOLD HIM YOU WERE COMING.

HIS ANSWER WAS 'THE WORSE.'

BACK, EDMUND, TO MY BROTHER. THIS KISS, IF IT DURST SPEAK, WOULD STRETCH THY SPIRITS UP INTO THE AIR.

25

Enter Albany...

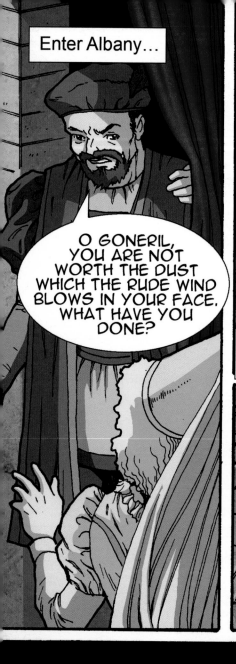

O GONERIL, YOU ARE NOT WORTH THE DUST WHICH THE RUDE WIND BLOWS IN YOUR FACE. WHAT HAVE YOU DONE?

TIGERS, NOT DAUGHTERS, WHAT HAVE YOU PERFORMED? A FATHER, AND A GRACIOUS AGED MAN HAVE YOU MADDED.

WHERE'S THY DRUM? FRANCE SPREADS HIS BANNERS IN OUR NOISELESS LAND, WITH PLUMED HELM THY STATE BEGINS TO THREAT.

A Messenger interrupts with news.

O MY GOOD LORD, THE DUKE OF CORNWALL'S DEAD, SLAIN BY HIS SERVANT, GOING TO PUT OUT THE OTHER EYE OF GLOUCESTER.

THIS SHOWS YOU ARE ABOVE, YOU JUSTICERS, THAT THESE OUR NETHER CRIMES SO SPEEDILY CAN VENGE!

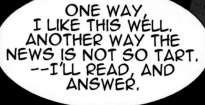

ONE WAY, I LIKE THIS WELL. ANOTHER WAY THE NEWS IS NOT SO TART. --I'LL READ, AND ANSWER.

In Dover…

WHY THE KING OF FRANCE IS SO SUDDENLY GONE BACK KNOW YOU THE REASON?

SOMETHING HE LEFT IMPERFECT IN THE STATE, WHICH IMPORTS TO THE KINGDOM SO MUCH FEAR AND DANGER THAT HIS PERSONAL RETURN WAS MOST REQUIRED AND NECESSARY.

DID YOUR LETTERS PIERCE THE QUEEN TO ANY DEMONSTRATION OF GRIEF?

AY, SIR, SHE TOOK THEM, READ THEM IN MY PRESENCE…

…AND NOW AND THEN AN AMPLE TEAR TRILLED DOWN HER DELICATE CHEEK.

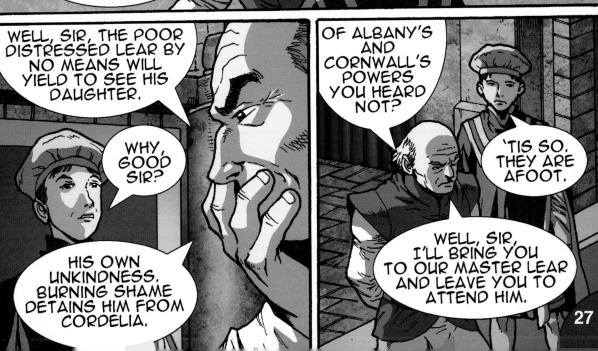

WELL, SIR, THE POOR DISTRESSED LEAR BY NO MEANS WILL YIELD TO SEE HIS DAUGHTER.

WHY, GOOD SIR?

HIS OWN UNKINDNESS. BURNING SHAME DETAINS HIM FROM CORDELIA.

OF ALBANY'S AND CORNWALL'S POWERS YOU HEARD NOT?

'TIS SO. THEY ARE AFOOT.

WELL, SIR, I'LL BRING YOU TO OUR MASTER LEAR AND LEAVE YOU TO ATTEND HIM.

27

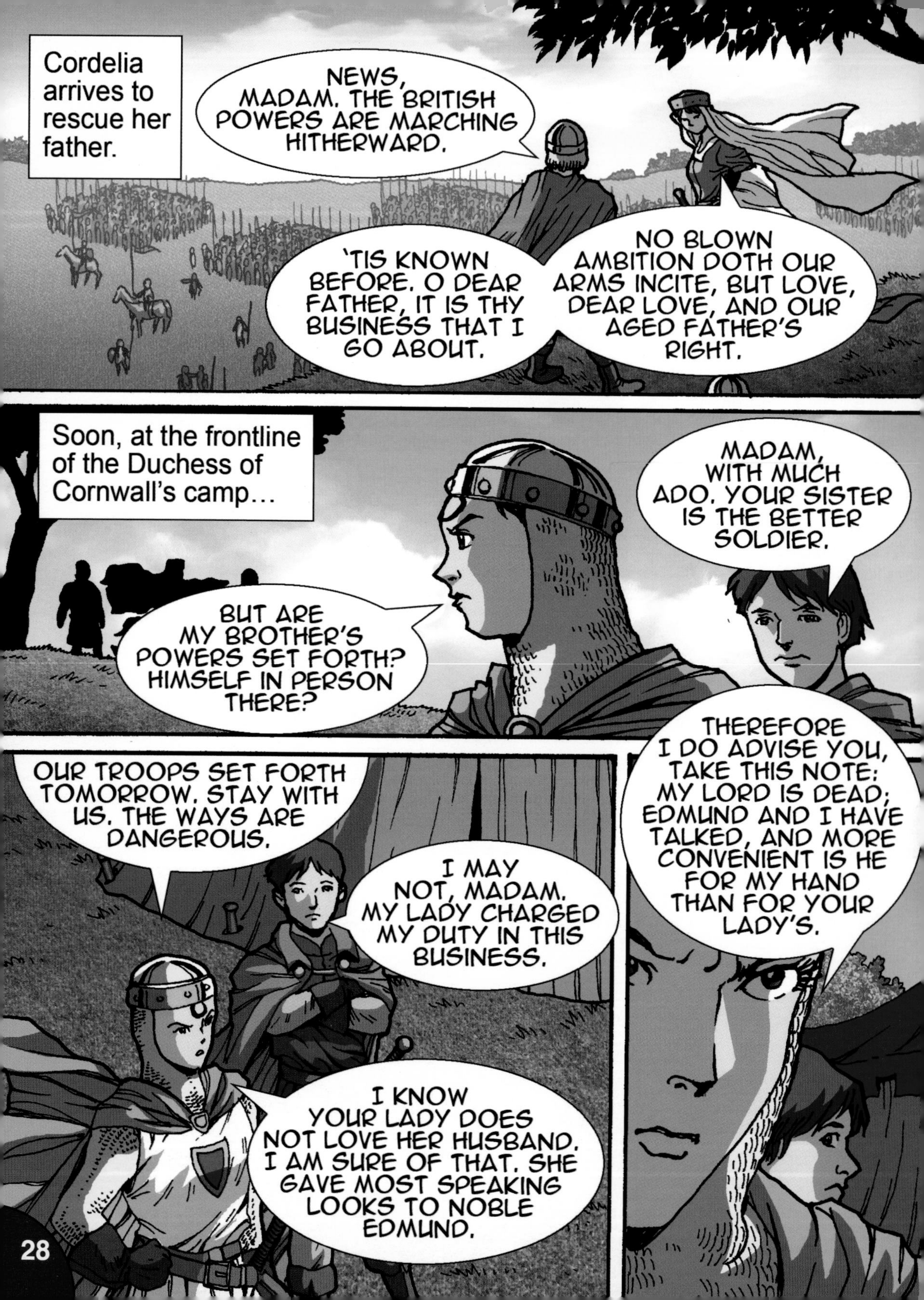
Cordelia arrives to rescue her father.
NEWS, MADAM. THE BRITISH POWERS ARE MARCHING HITHERWARD.
'TIS KNOWN BEFORE. O DEAR FATHER, IT IS THY BUSINESS THAT I GO ABOUT.
NO BLOWN AMBITION DOTH OUR ARMS INCITE, BUT LOVE, DEAR LOVE, AND OUR AGED FATHER'S RIGHT.
Soon, at the frontline of the Duchess of Cornwall's camp…
BUT ARE MY BROTHER'S POWERS SET FORTH? HIMSELF IN PERSON THERE?
MADAM, WITH MUCH ADO. YOUR SISTER IS THE BETTER SOLDIER.
OUR TROOPS SET FORTH TOMORROW. STAY WITH US. THE WAYS ARE DANGEROUS.
I MAY NOT, MADAM. MY LADY CHARGED MY DUTY IN THIS BUSINESS.
I KNOW YOUR LADY DOES NOT LOVE HER HUSBAND. I AM SURE OF THAT. SHE GAVE MOST SPEAKING LOOKS TO NOBLE EDMUND.
THEREFORE I DO ADVISE YOU, TAKE THIS NOTE: MY LORD IS DEAD; EDMUND AND I HAVE TALKED, AND MORE CONVENIENT IS HE FOR MY HAND THAN FOR YOUR LADY'S.

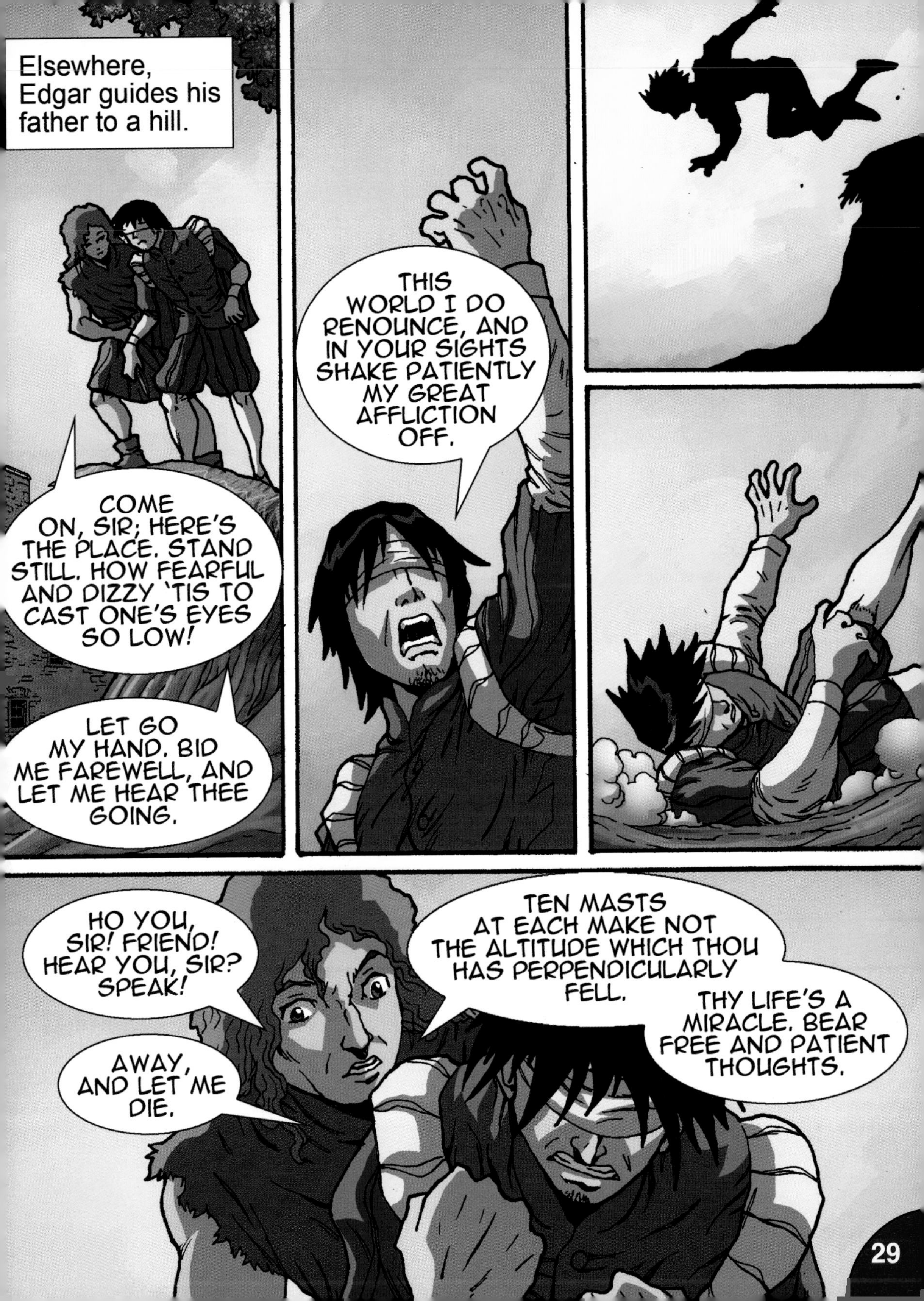

Elsewhere, Edgar guides his father to a hill.
COME ON, SIR; HERE'S THE PLACE. STAND STILL. HOW FEARFUL AND DIZZY 'TIS TO CAST ONE'S EYES SO LOW!
LET GO MY HAND. BID ME FAREWELL, AND LET ME HEAR THEE GOING.
THIS WORLD I DO RENOUNCE, AND IN YOUR SIGHTS SHAKE PATIENTLY MY GREAT AFFLICTION OFF.
HO YOU, SIR! FRIEND! HEAR YOU, SIR? SPEAK!
AWAY, AND LET ME DIE.
TEN MASTS AT EACH MAKE NOT THE ALTITUDE WHICH THOU HAS PERPENDICULARLY FELL.
THY LIFE'S A MIRACLE. BEAR FREE AND PATIENT THOUGHTS.

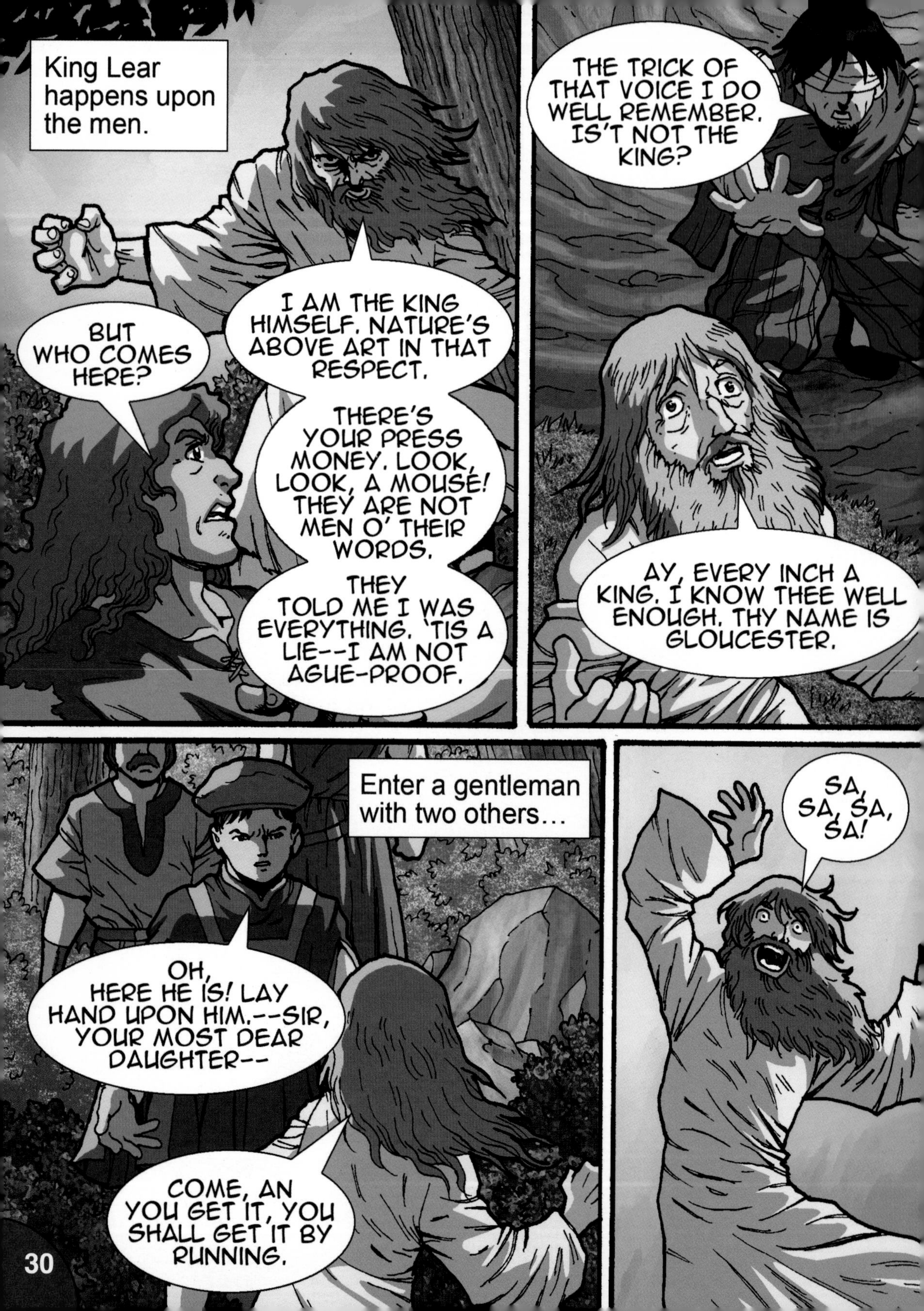
King Lear happens upon the men.
BUT WHO COMES HERE?
I AM THE KING HIMSELF. NATURE'S ABOVE ART IN THAT RESPECT.
THERE'S YOUR PRESS MONEY. LOOK, LOOK, A MOUSE! THEY ARE NOT MEN O' THEIR WORDS.
THEY TOLD ME I WAS EVERYTHING. 'TIS A LIE--I AM NOT AGUE-PROOF.
THE TRICK OF THAT VOICE I DO WELL REMEMBER. IS'T NOT THE KING?
AY, EVERY INCH A KING. I KNOW THEE WELL ENOUGH. THY NAME IS GLOUCESTER.
Enter a gentleman with two others…
OH, HERE HE IS! LAY HAND UPON HIM.--SIR, YOUR MOST DEAR DAUGHTER--
COME, AN YOU GET IT, YOU SHALL GET IT BY RUNNING.
SA, SA, SA, SA!

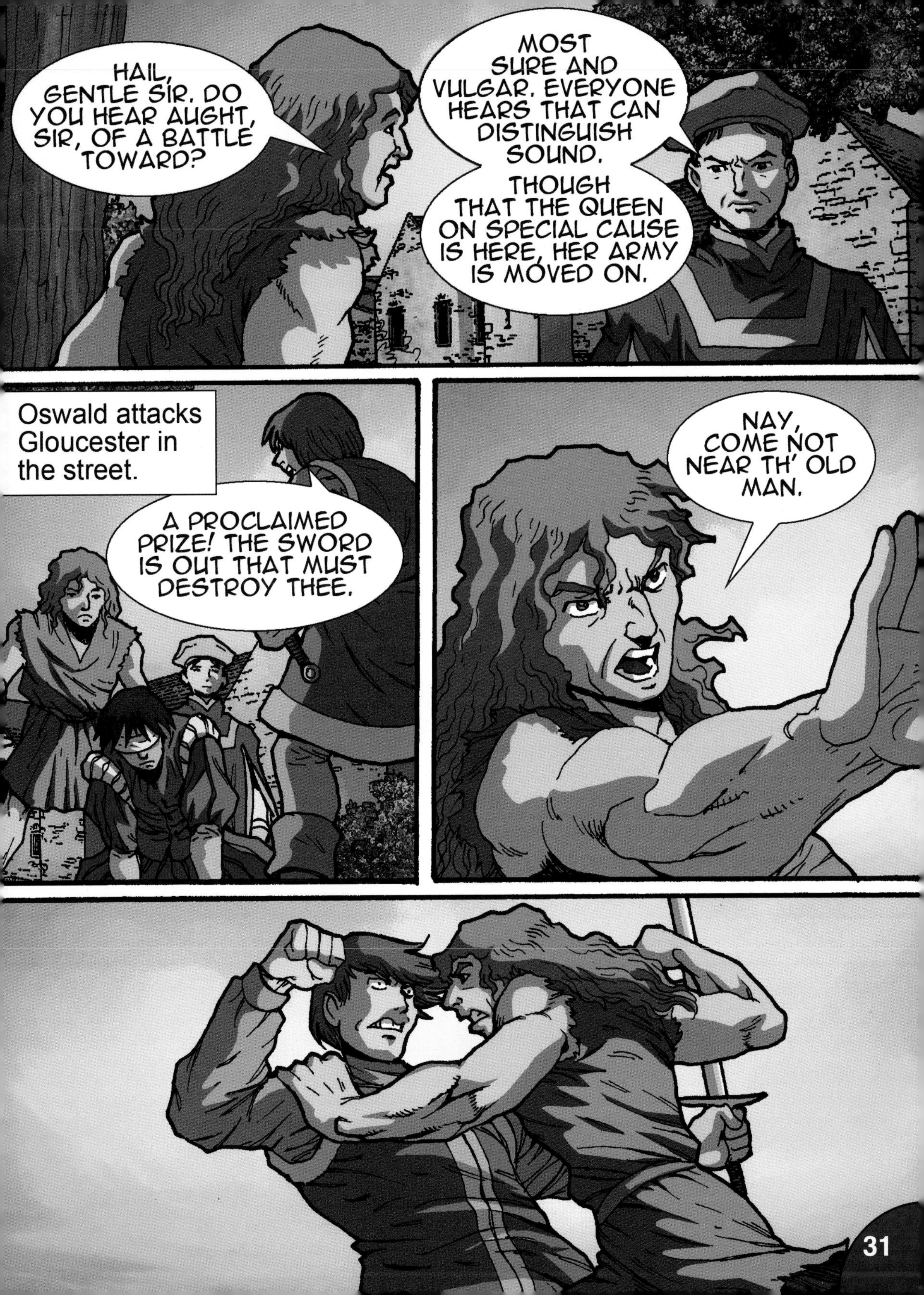
HAIL, GENTLE SIR. DO YOU HEAR AUGHT, SIR, OF A BATTLE TOWARD?
MOST SURE AND VULGAR. EVERYONE HEARS THAT CAN DISTINGUISH SOUND.
THOUGH THAT THE QUEEN ON SPECIAL CAUSE IS HERE, HER ARMY IS MOVED ON.
Oswald attacks Gloucester in the street.
A PROCLAIMED PRIZE! THE SWORD IS OUT THAT MUST DESTROY THEE.
NAY, COME NOT NEAR TH' OLD MAN.
31

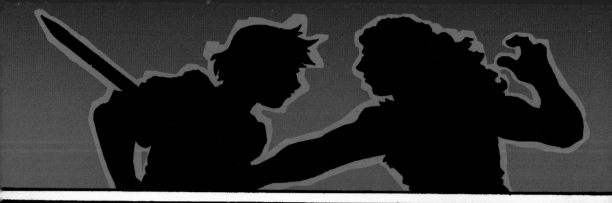

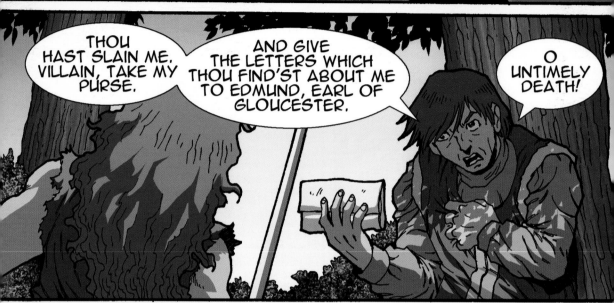

THOU HAST SLAIN ME. VILLAIN, TAKE MY PURSE.

AND GIVE THE LETTERS WHICH THOU FIND'ST ABOUT ME TO EDMUND, EARL OF GLOUCESTER.

O UNTIMELY DEATH!

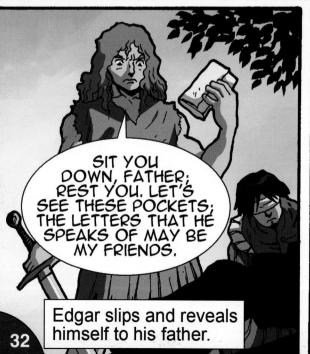

SIT YOU DOWN, FATHER; REST YOU. LET'S SEE THESE POCKETS; THE LETTERS THAT HE SPEAKS OF MAY BE MY FRIENDS.

Edgar slips and reveals himself to his father.

In the letters, Edgar reads of Goneril's plot to kill her husband.

A PLOT UPON HER VIRTUOUS HUSBAND'S LIFE, AND THE EXCHANGE MY BROTHER! COME, FATHER, I'LL BESTOW YOU WITH A FRIEND.

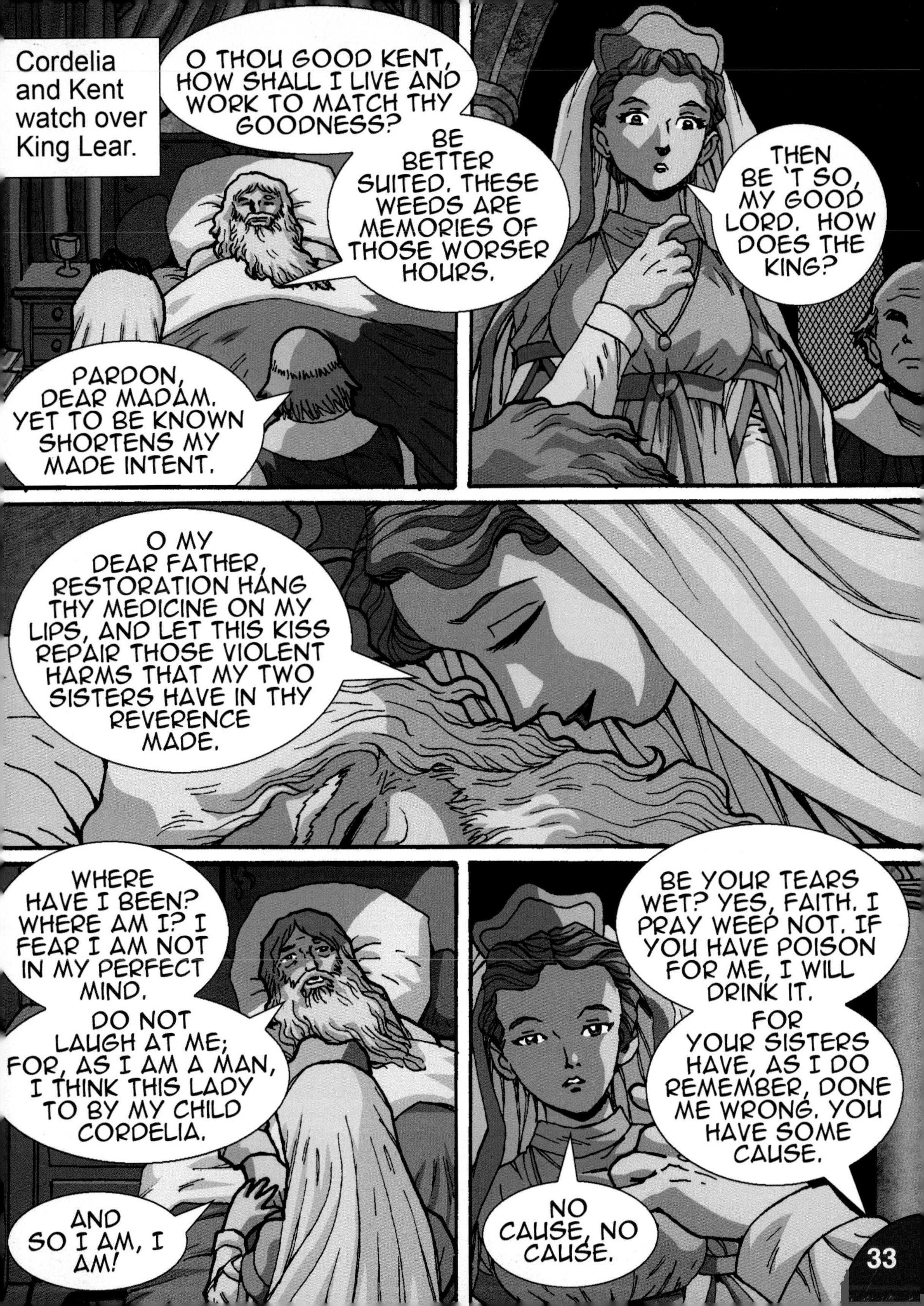

Cordelia and Kent watch over King Lear.
O THOU GOOD KENT, HOW SHALL I LIVE AND WORK TO MATCH THY GOODNESS?
BE BETTER SUITED. THESE WEEDS ARE MEMORIES OF THOSE WORSER HOURS.
PARDON, DEAR MADAM. YET TO BE KNOWN SHORTENS MY MADE INTENT.
THEN BE 'T SO, MY GOOD LORD. HOW DOES THE KING?
O MY DEAR FATHER, RESTORATION HANG THY MEDICINE ON MY LIPS, AND LET THIS KISS REPAIR THOSE VIOLENT HARMS THAT MY TWO SISTERS HAVE IN THY REVERENCE MADE.
WHERE HAVE I BEEN? WHERE AM I? I FEAR I AM NOT IN MY PERFECT MIND.
DO NOT LAUGH AT ME; FOR, AS I AM A MAN, I THINK THIS LADY TO BY MY CHILD CORDELIA.
AND SO I AM, I AM!
BE YOUR TEARS WET? YES, FAITH. I PRAY WEEP NOT. IF YOU HAVE POISON FOR ME, I WILL DRINK IT.
FOR YOUR SISTERS HAVE, AS I DO REMEMBER, DONE ME WRONG. YOU HAVE SOME CAUSE.
NO CAUSE, NO CAUSE.

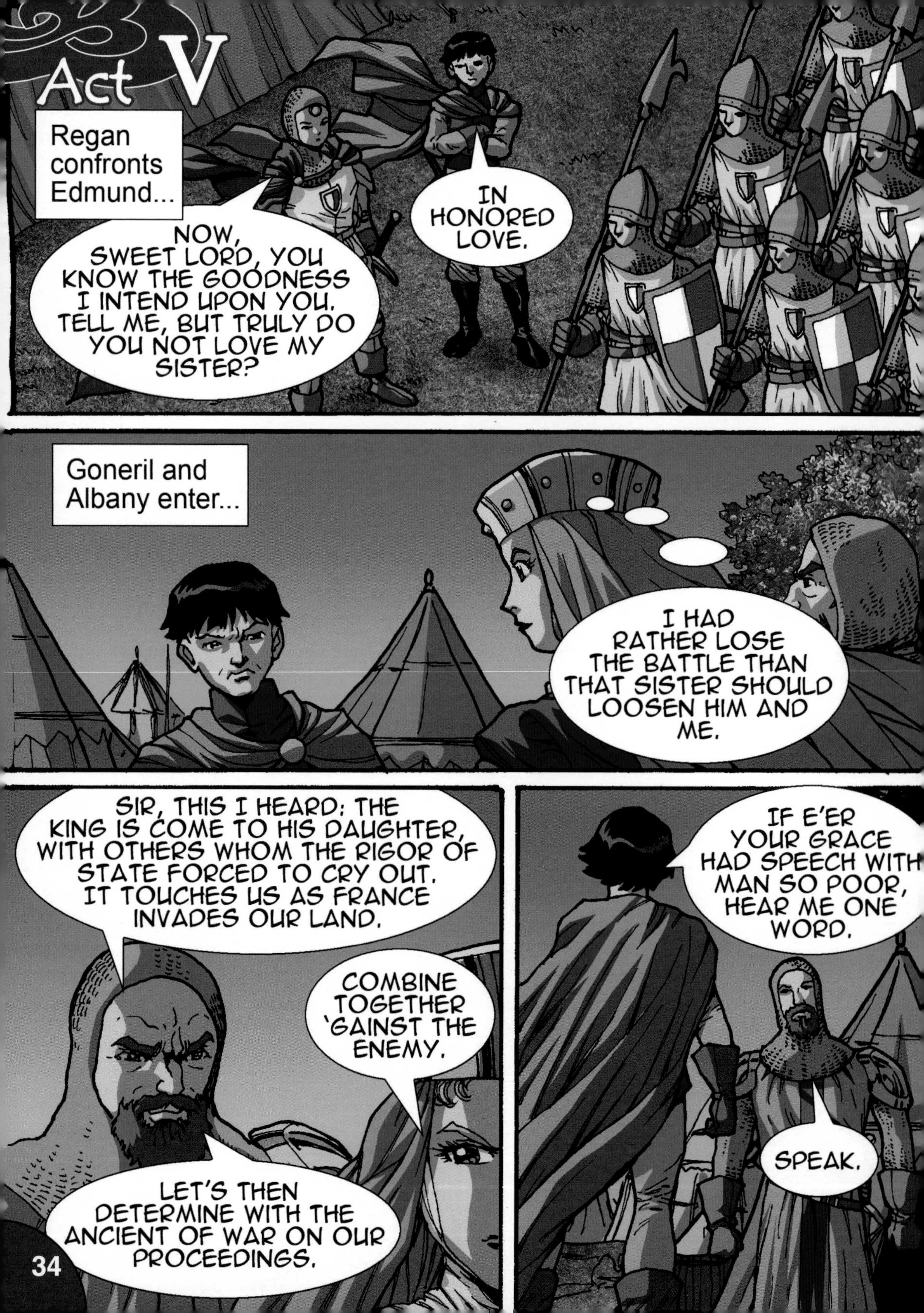
Act V
Regan confronts Edmund...
NOW, SWEET LORD, YOU KNOW THE GOODNESS I INTEND UPON YOU. TELL ME, BUT TRULY DO YOU NOT LOVE MY SISTER?
IN HONORED LOVE.
Goneril and Albany enter...
I HAD RATHER LOSE THE BATTLE THAN THAT SISTER SHOULD LOOSEN HIM AND ME.
SIR, THIS I HEARD: THE KING IS COME TO HIS DAUGHTER, WITH OTHERS WHOM THE RIGOR OF STATE FORCED TO CRY OUT. IT TOUCHES US AS FRANCE INVADES OUR LAND.
COMBINE TOGETHER 'GAINST THE ENEMY.
LET'S THEN DETERMINE WITH THE ANCIENT OF WAR ON OUR PROCEEDINGS.
IF E'ER YOUR GRACE HAD SPEECH WITH MAN SO POOR, HEAR ME ONE WORD.
SPEAK.

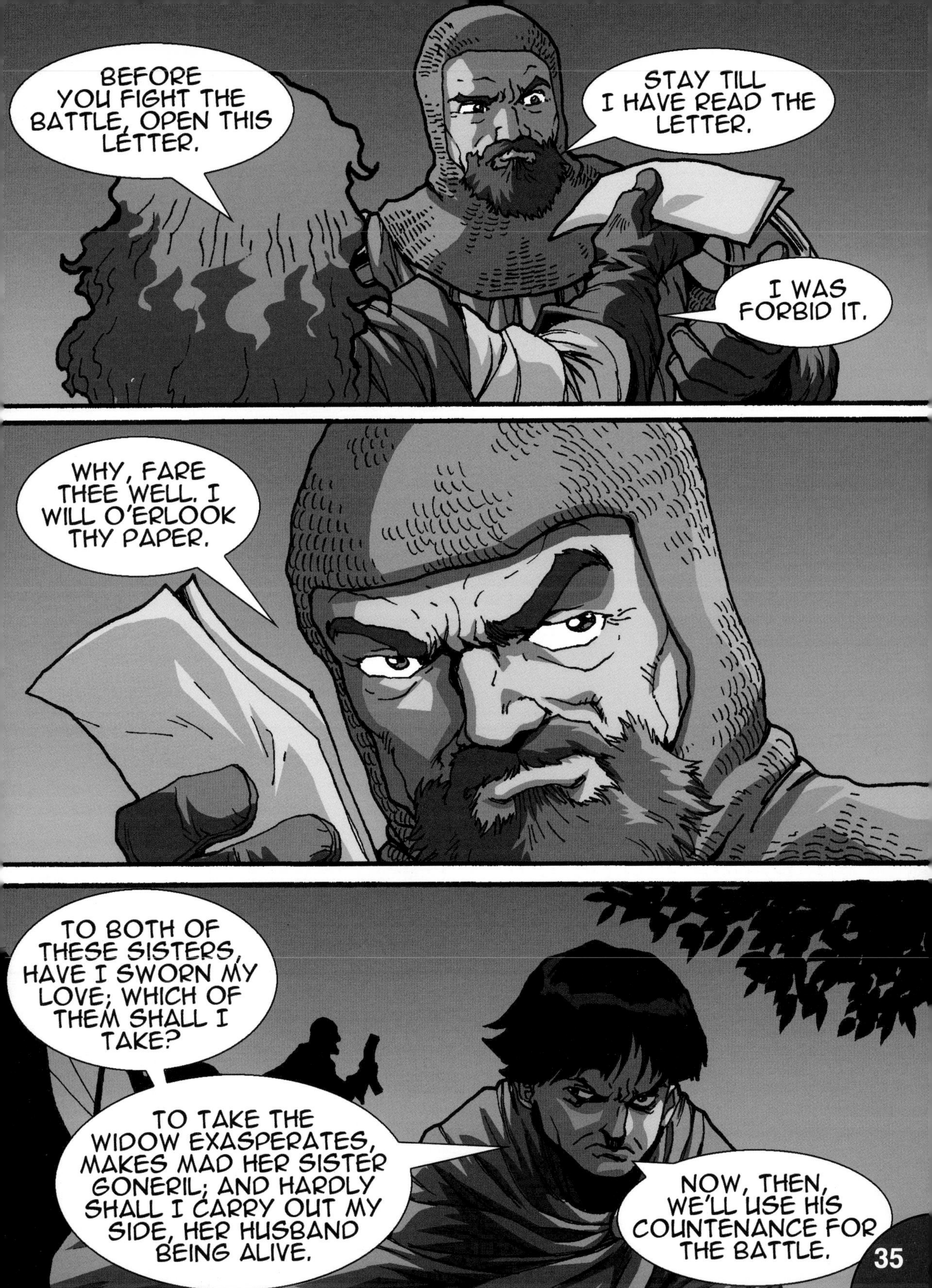
BEFORE YOU FIGHT THE BATTLE, OPEN THIS LETTER.
STAY TILL I HAVE READ THE LETTER.
I WAS FORBID IT.
WHY, FARE THEE WELL. I WILL O'ERLOOK THY PAPER.
TO BOTH OF THESE SISTERS, HAVE I SWORN MY LOVE; WHICH OF THEM SHALL I TAKE?
TO TAKE THE WIDOW EXASPERATES, MAKES MAD HER SISTER GONERIL; AND HARDLY SHALL I CARRY OUT MY SIDE, HER HUSBAND BEING ALIVE.
NOW, THEN, WE'LL USE HIS COUNTENANCE FOR THE BATTLE.

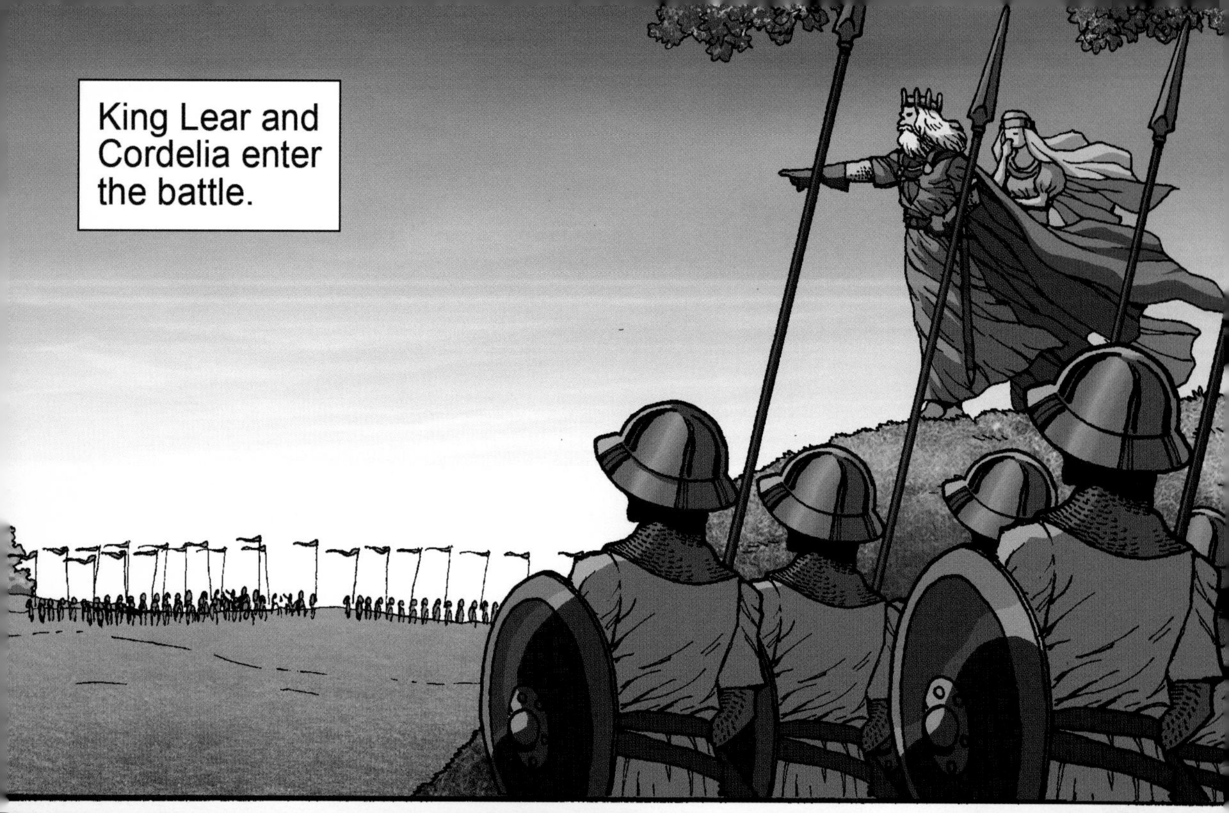
King Lear and Cordelia enter the battle.

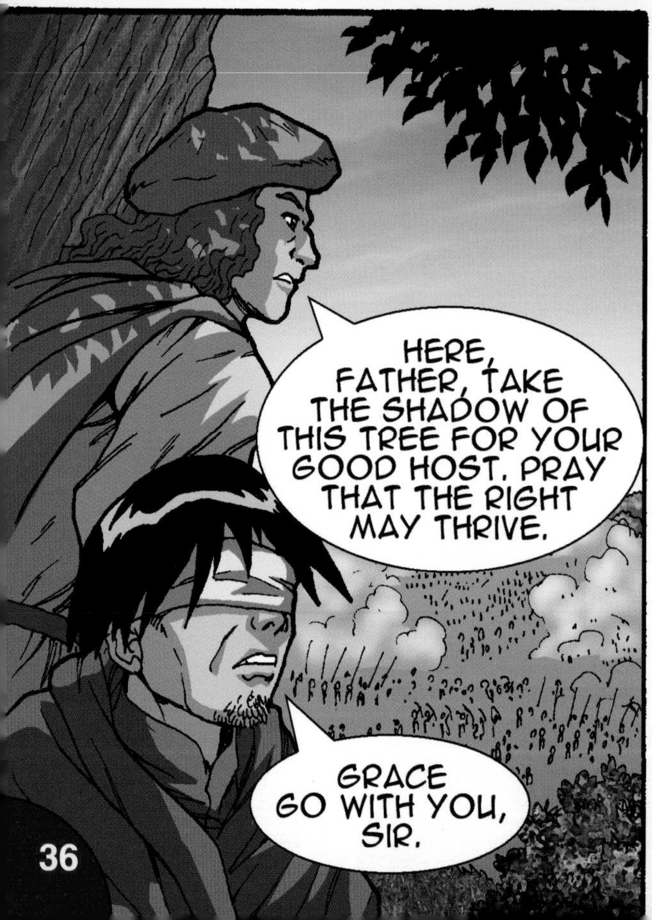
HERE, FATHER, TAKE THE SHADOW OF THIS TREE FOR YOUR GOOD HOST. PRAY THAT THE RIGHT MAY THRIVE.
GRACE GO WITH YOU, SIR.

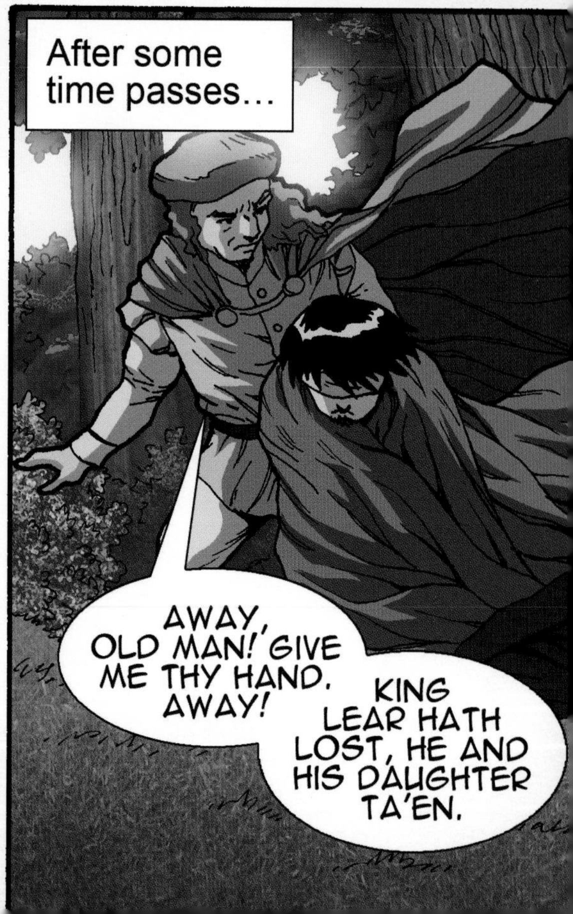
After some time passes…
AWAY, OLD MAN! GIVE ME THY HAND. AWAY!
KING LEAR HATH LOST, HE AND HIS DAUGHTER TA'EN.

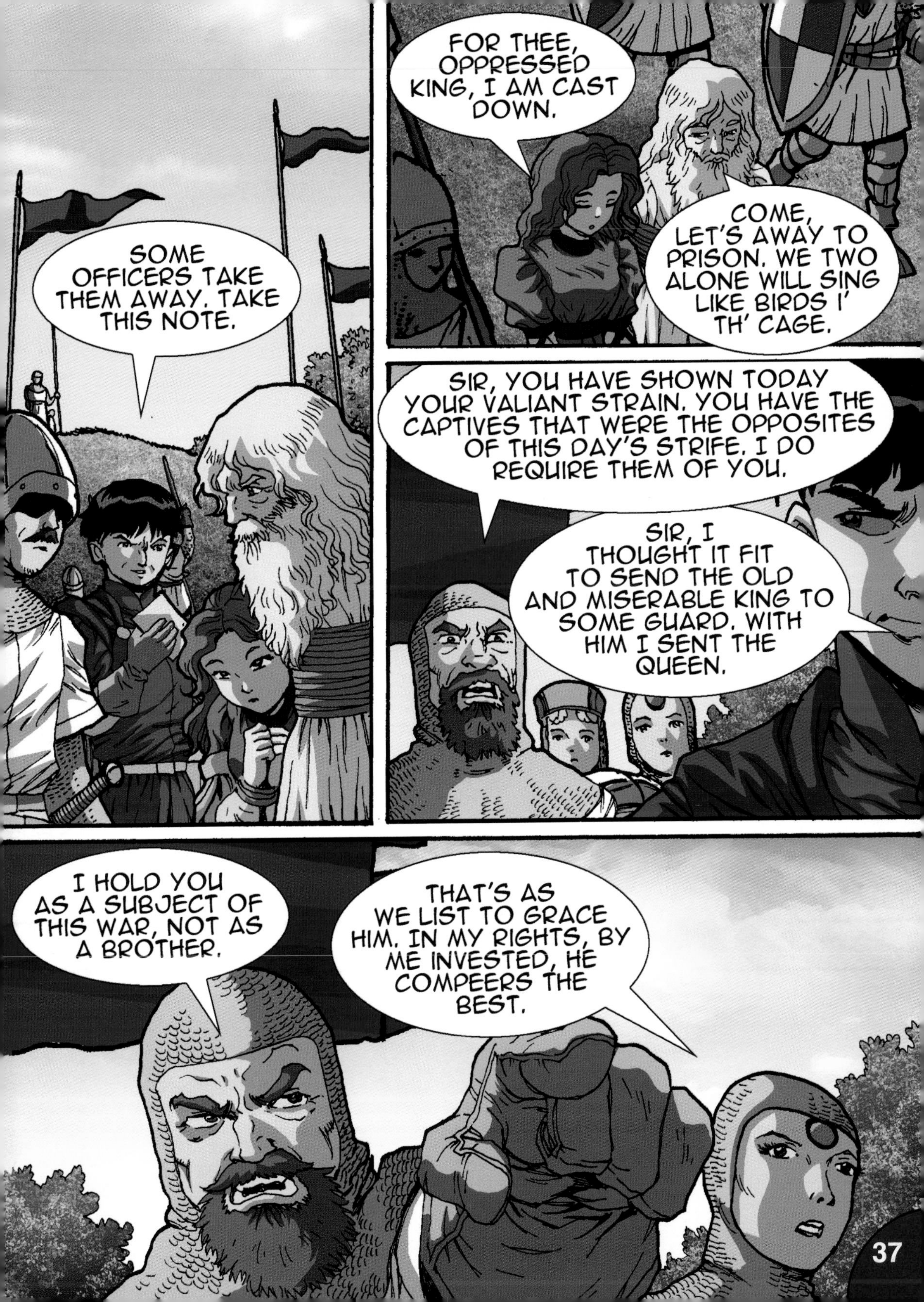
SOME OFFICERS TAKE THEM AWAY. TAKE THIS NOTE.
FOR THEE, OPPRESSED KING, I AM CAST DOWN.
COME, LET'S AWAY TO PRISON. WE TWO ALONE WILL SING LIKE BIRDS I' TH' CAGE.
SIR, YOU HAVE SHOWN TODAY YOUR VALIANT STRAIN. YOU HAVE THE CAPTIVES THAT WERE THE OPPOSITES OF THIS DAY'S STRIFE. I DO REQUIRE THEM OF YOU.
SIR, I THOUGHT IT FIT TO SEND THE OLD AND MISERABLE KING TO SOME GUARD. WITH HIM I SENT THE QUEEN.
I HOLD YOU AS A SUBJECT OF THIS WAR, NOT AS A BROTHER.
THAT'S AS WE LIST TO GRACE HIM. IN MY RIGHTS, BY ME INVESTED, HE COMPEERS THE BEST.

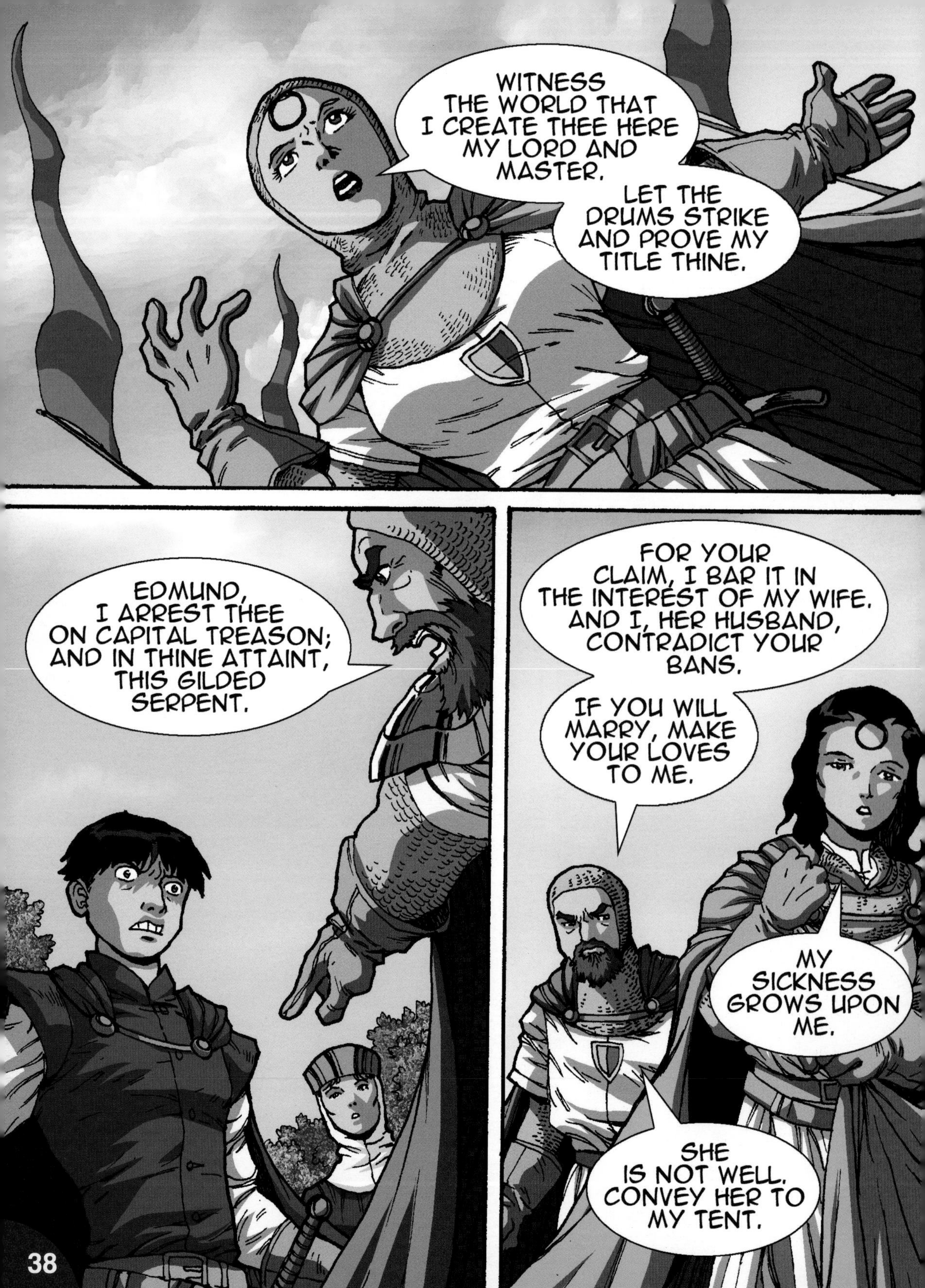
WITNESS THE WORLD THAT I CREATE THEE HERE MY LORD AND MASTER.
LET THE DRUMS STRIKE AND PROVE MY TITLE THINE.
EDMUND, I ARREST THEE ON CAPITAL TREASON; AND IN THINE ATTAINT, THIS GILDED SERPENT.
FOR YOUR CLAIM, I BAR IT IN THE INTEREST OF MY WIFE. AND I, HER HUSBAND, CONTRADICT YOUR BANS.
IF YOU WILL MARRY, MAKE YOUR LOVES TO ME.
MY SICKNESS GROWS UPON ME.
SHE IS NOT WELL. CONVEY HER TO MY TENT.

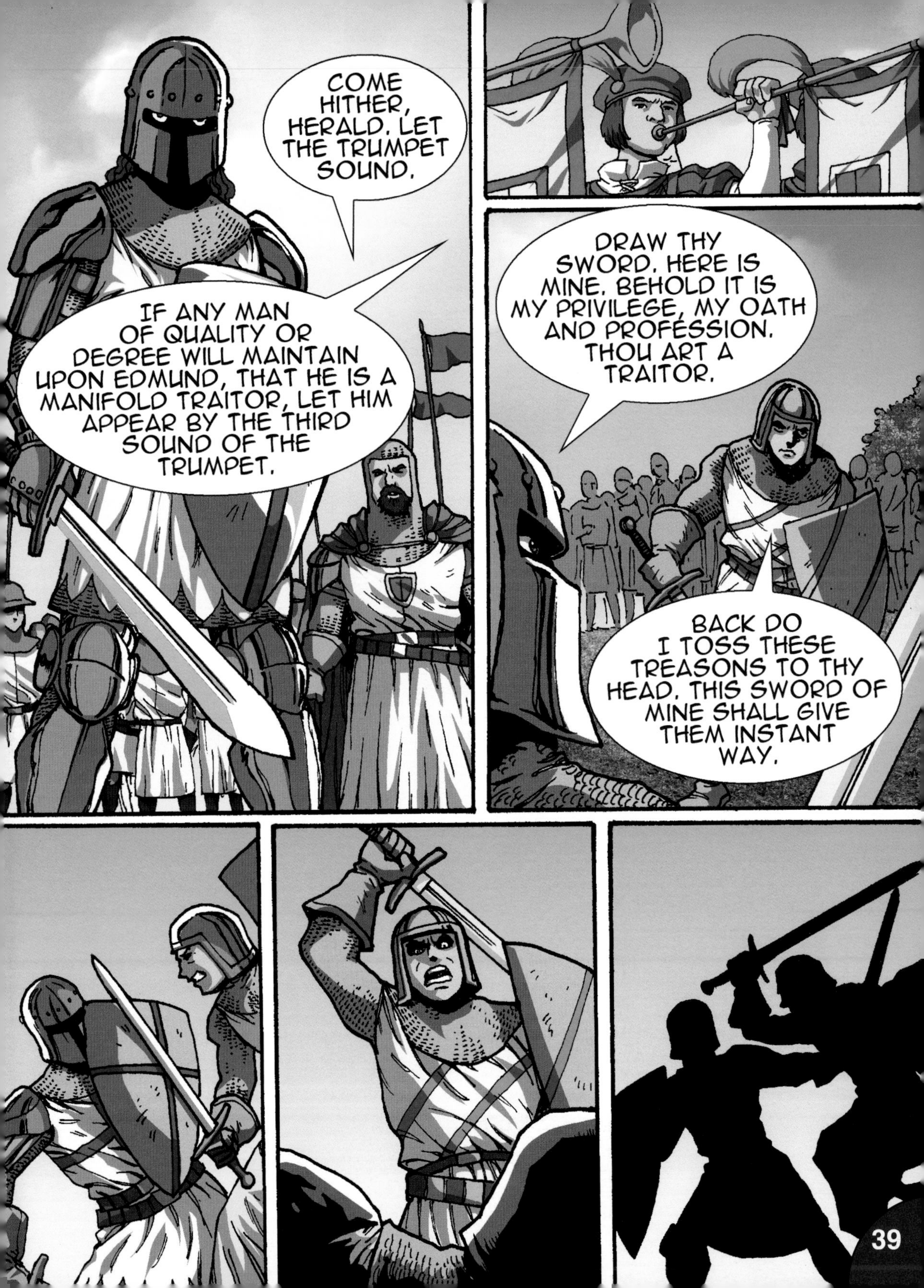
COME HITHER, HERALD. LET THE TRUMPET SOUND.
IF ANY MAN OF QUALITY OR DEGREE WILL MAINTAIN UPON EDMUND, THAT HE IS A MANIFOLD TRAITOR, LET HIM APPEAR BY THE THIRD SOUND OF THE TRUMPET.
DRAW THY SWORD. HERE IS MINE. BEHOLD IT IS MY PRIVILEGE, MY OATH AND PROFESSION. THOU ART A TRAITOR.
BACK DO I TOSS THESE TREASONS TO THY HEAD. THIS SWORD OF MINE SHALL GIVE THEM INSTANT WAY.

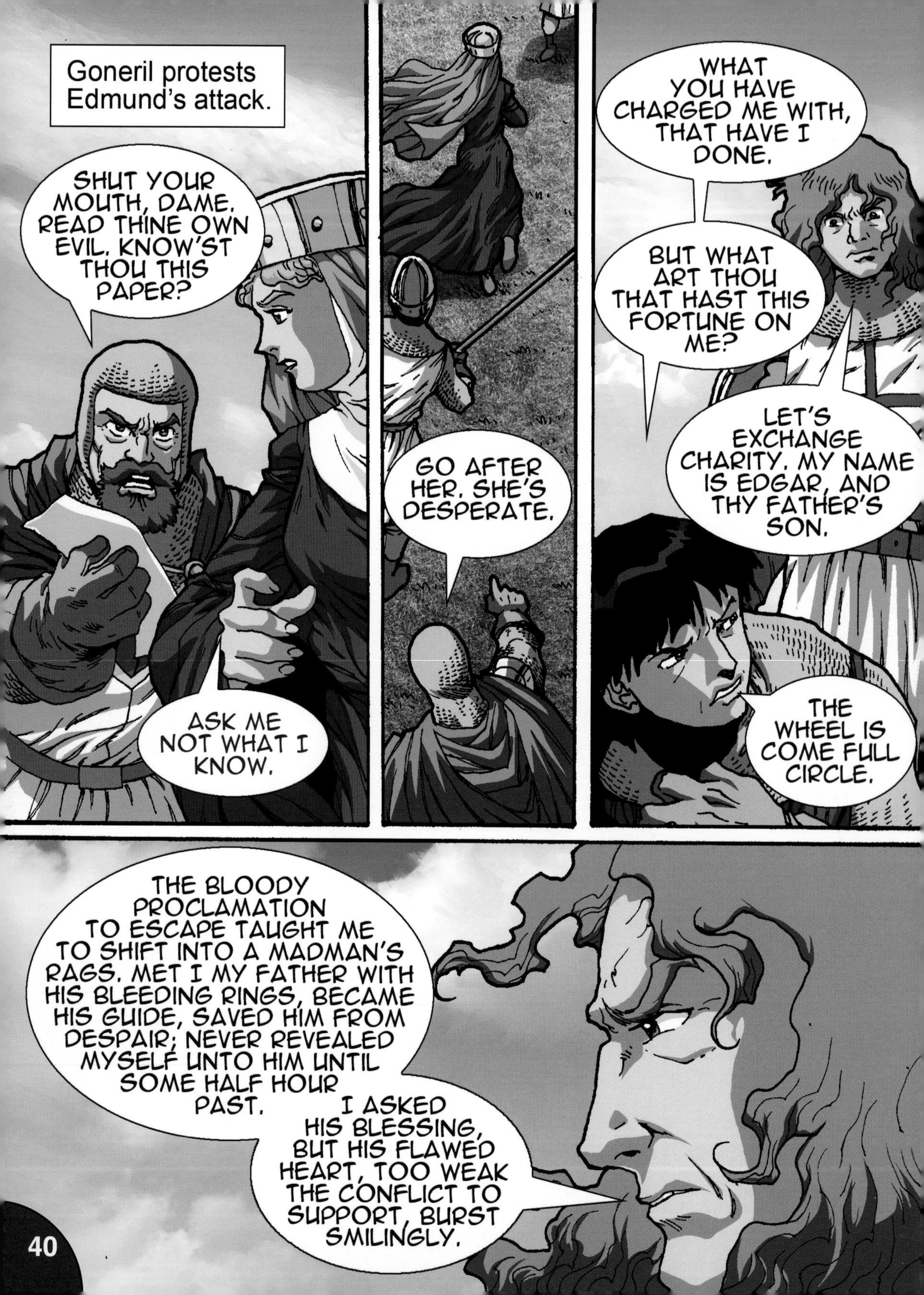
Goneril protests Edmund's attack.
SHUT YOUR MOUTH, DAME. READ THINE OWN EVIL. KNOW'ST THOU THIS PAPER?
ASK ME NOT WHAT I KNOW.
GO AFTER HER. SHE'S DESPERATE.
WHAT YOU HAVE CHARGED ME WITH, THAT HAVE I DONE.
BUT WHAT ART THOU THAT HAST THIS FORTUNE ON ME?
LET'S EXCHANGE CHARITY. MY NAME IS EDGAR, AND THY FATHER'S SON.
THE WHEEL IS COME FULL CIRCLE.
THE BLOODY PROCLAMATION TO ESCAPE TAUGHT ME TO SHIFT INTO A MADMAN'S RAGS. MET I MY FATHER WITH HIS BLEEDING RINGS, BECAME HIS GUIDE, SAVED HIM FROM DESPAIR; NEVER REVEALED MYSELF UNTO HIM UNTIL SOME HALF HOUR PAST.
I ASKED HIS BLESSING, BUT HIS FLAWED HEART, TOO WEAK THE CONFLICT TO SUPPORT, BURST SMILINGLY.

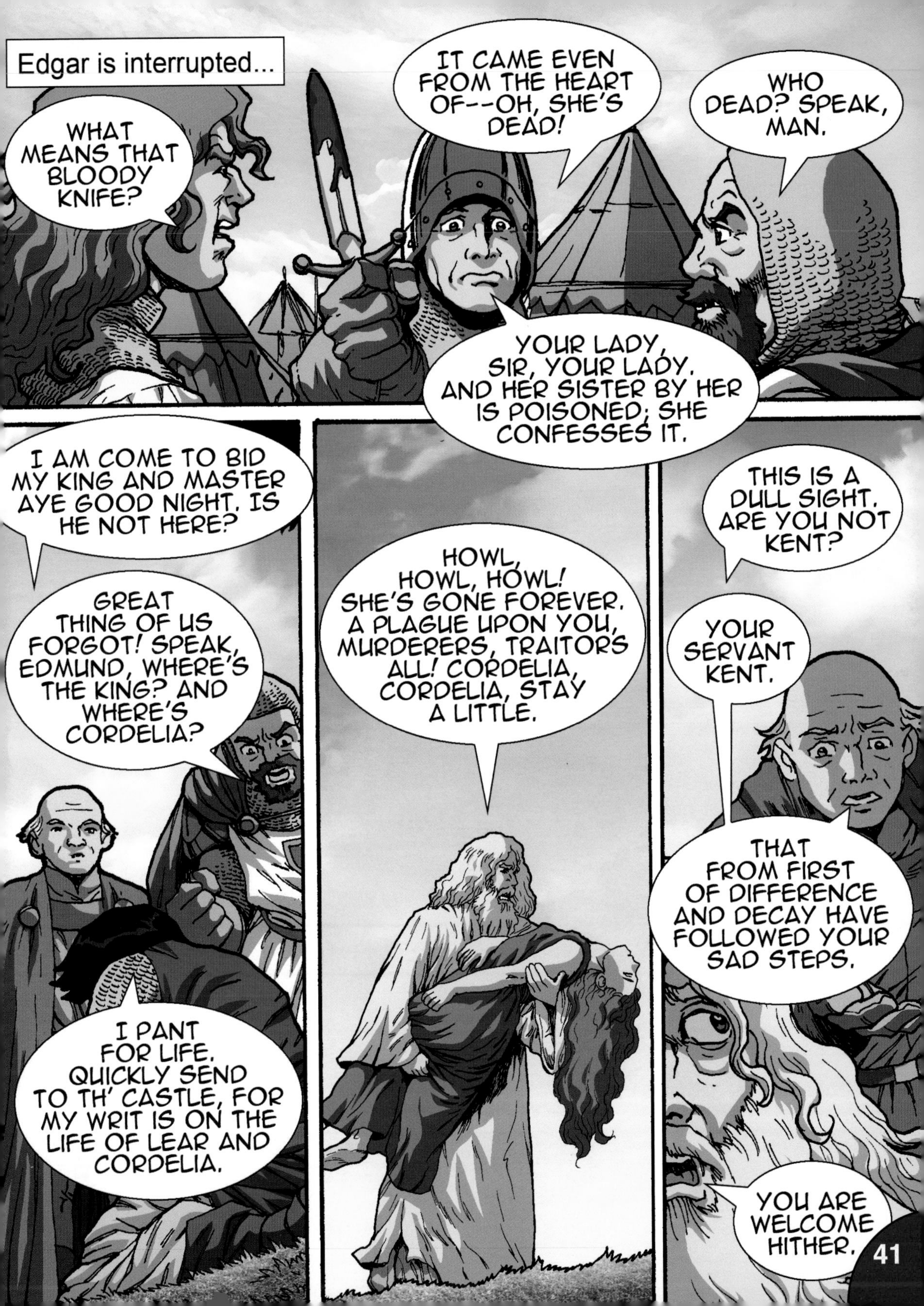
Edgar is interrupted...
WHAT MEANS THAT BLOODY KNIFE?
IT CAME EVEN FROM THE HEART OF--OH, SHE'S DEAD!
WHO DEAD? SPEAK, MAN.
YOUR LADY, SIR, YOUR LADY. AND HER SISTER BY HER IS POISONED; SHE CONFESSES IT.
I AM COME TO BID MY KING AND MASTER AYE GOOD NIGHT. IS HE NOT HERE?
GREAT THING OF US FORGOT! SPEAK, EDMUND, WHERE'S THE KING? AND WHERE'S CORDELIA?
I PANT FOR LIFE. QUICKLY SEND TO TH' CASTLE, FOR MY WRIT IS ON THE LIFE OF LEAR AND CORDELIA.
HOWL, HOWL, HOWL! SHE'S GONE FOREVER. A PLAGUE UPON YOU, MURDERERS, TRAITORS ALL! CORDELIA, CORDELIA, STAY A LITTLE.
THIS IS A DULL SIGHT. ARE YOU NOT KENT?
YOUR SERVANT KENT.
THAT FROM FIRST OF DIFFERENCE AND DECAY HAVE FOLLOWED YOUR SAD STEPS.
YOU ARE WELCOME HITHER.

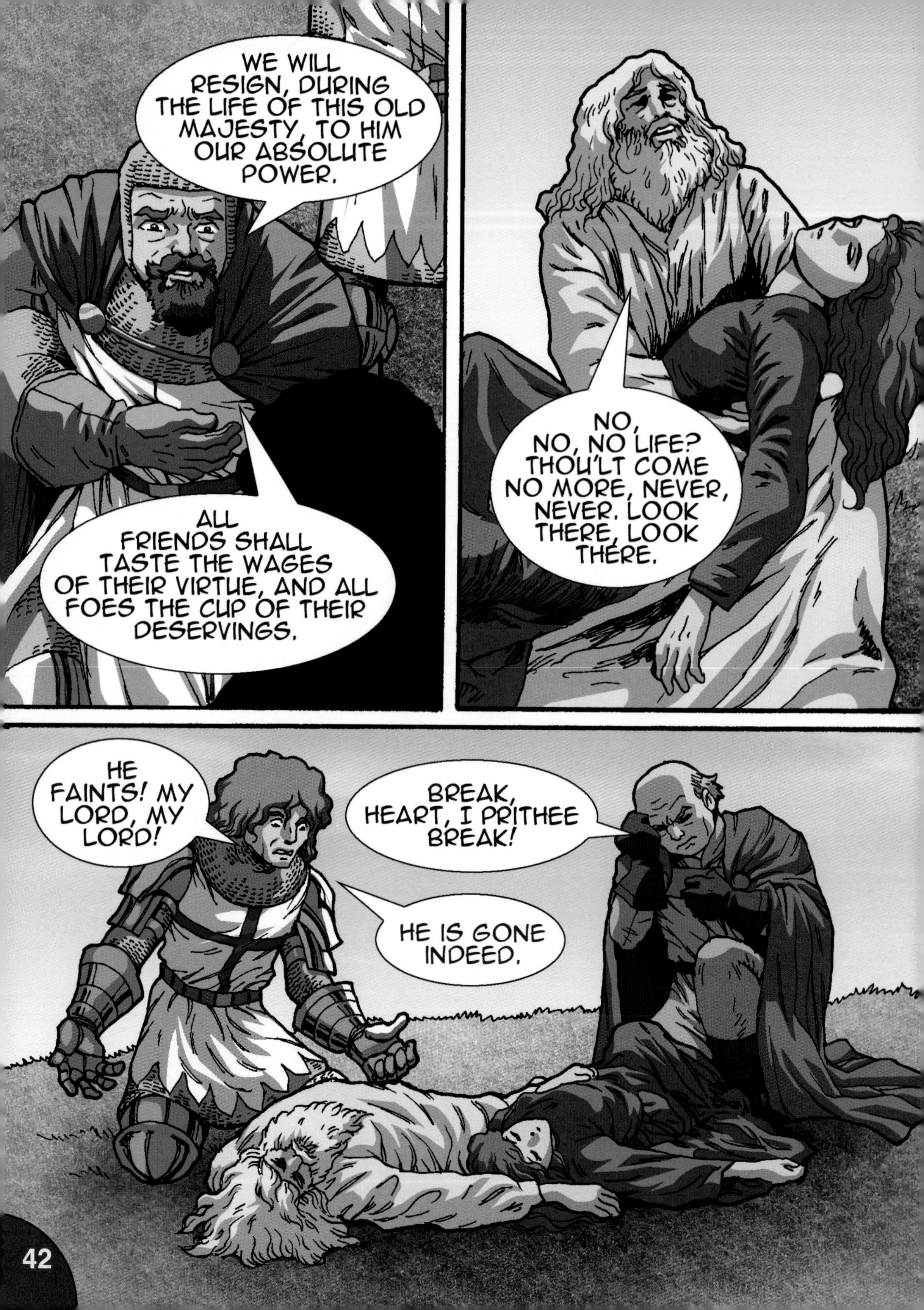
WE WILL RESIGN, DURING THE LIFE OF THIS OLD MAJESTY, TO HIM OUR ABSOLUTE POWER.
ALL FRIENDS SHALL TASTE THE WAGES OF THEIR VIRTUE, AND ALL FOES THE CUP OF THEIR DESERVINGS.
NO, NO, NO LIFE? THOU'LT COME NO MORE, NEVER, NEVER. LOOK THERE, LOOK THERE.
HE FAINTS! MY LORD, MY LORD!
BREAK, HEART, I PRITHEE BREAK!
HE IS GONE INDEED.

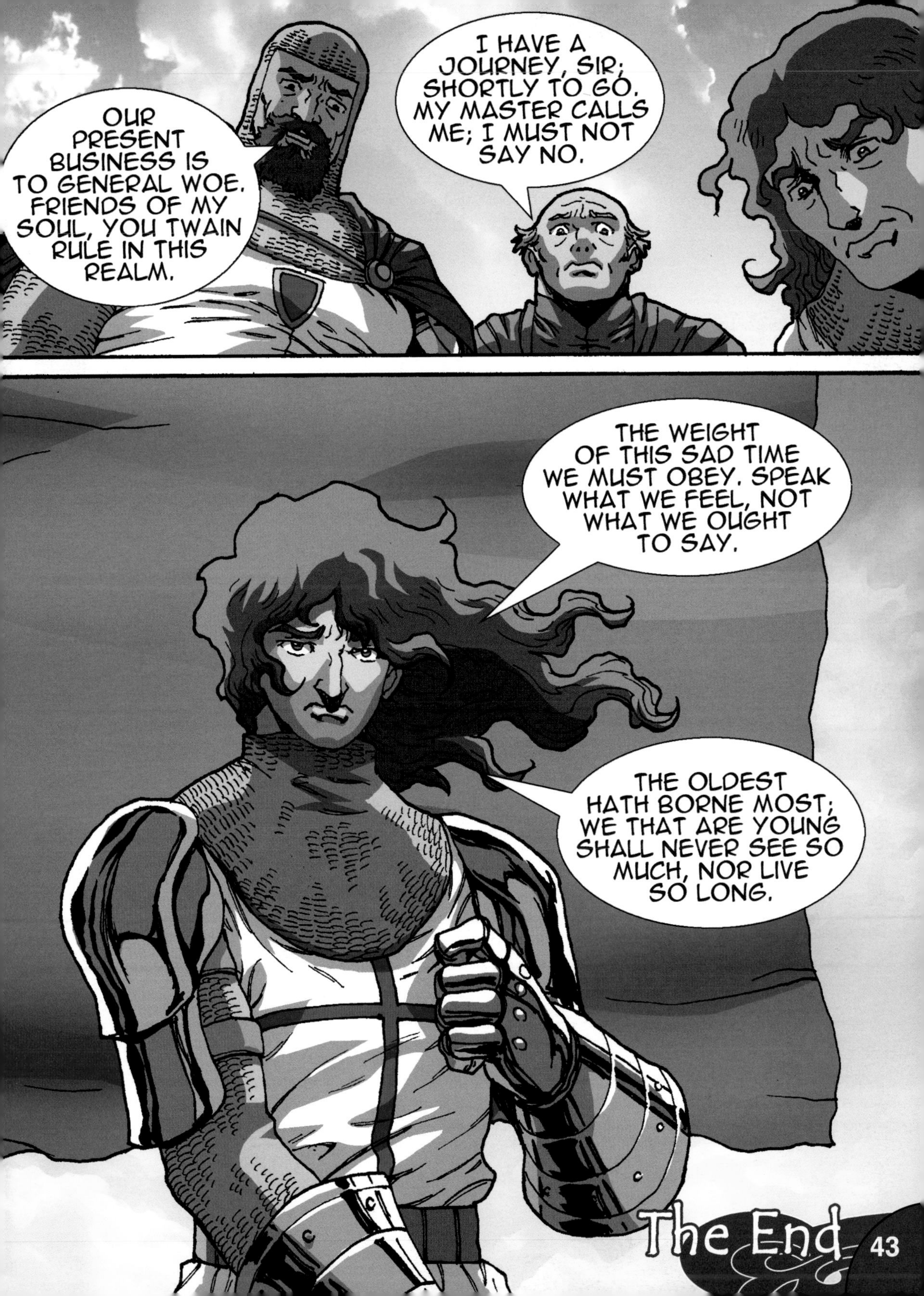
OUR PRESENT BUSINESS IS TO GENERAL WOE. FRIENDS OF MY SOUL, YOU TWAIN RULE IN THIS REALM.
I HAVE A JOURNEY, SIR; SHORTLY TO GO. MY MASTER CALLS ME; I MUST NOT SAY NO.
THE WEIGHT OF THIS SAD TIME WE MUST OBEY. SPEAK WHAT WE FEEL, NOT WHAT WE OUGHT TO SAY.
THE OLDEST HATH BORNE MOST; WE THAT ARE YOUNG SHALL NEVER SEE SO MUCH, NOR LIVE SO LONG.
The End

Behind King Lear

King Lear was written in about 1605 to 1606. It was first printed in 1608 in the quarto. In 1623, it appeared in Shakespeare's *First Folio*. The five-act play that appears in the *First Folio* is very different from the one in the quarto. It appears that Shakespeare made changes that cut the length of the play.

King Lear opens with the king splitting his kingdom into three parts, one for each of his daughters. He then asks his children to tell him how much they love him to receive their share. His daughters Goneril and Regan proclaim their love. The youngest daughter, Cordelia, refuses to be insincere. King Lear disinherits her.

Goneril and Regan and their husbands now split the kingdom. They are to care for King Lear and his men at arms. But the daughters renege on their vows, so Lear becomes mad with grief and is left out in the storm with only his loyal servant Kent.

Meanwhile, the Earl of Gloucester has two sons, Edgar and Edmund. Edmund is illegitimate and cannot claim the title. He plots to have Edgar cast aside and romances Goneril and Regan to further his own place in the kingdom. Edgar is forced to disguise himself as a madman and becomes companion to Lear.

Cordelia learns of her father's neglect by her sisters and invades with the army of France. She finds her father and nurses him to health. But Cordelia and Lear are captured in the battle between France and England and are imprisoned.

Goneril is jealous of Regan's relationship with Edmund and poisons her sister. When Edmund is arrested for treason, Goneril then takes her own life. Goneril's husband, the Duke of Albany, tries to make things right, but is too late. Cordelia has died in custody and King Lear dies from a broken heart. The kingdom is left to Edgar to rule.

Since its beginning, *King Lear* has been performed onstage throughout the world. There are also both film and television adaptations of this famous play.

Be your tears wet?

The wheel is come full circle.

Things that love the night love not such nights as these.

'Tis strange that from their cold'st neglect my love should kindle to inflamed respect.

About the Author

William Shakespeare was baptized on April 26, 1564, in Stratford-upon-Avon, England. At the time, records were not kept of births, however, the churches did record baptisms, weddings, and deaths. So, we know approximately when he was born. Traditionally, his birth is celebrated on April 23.

William was the son of John Shakespeare, a tradesman, and Mary Arden. He most likely attended grammar school and learned to read, write, and speak Latin.

Shakespeare did not go on to the university. Instead, he married Anne Hathaway at age 18. They had three children, Susanna, Hamnet, and Judith. Not much is known about Shakespeare's life at this time. By 1592 he had moved to London, and his name began to appear in the literary world.

In 1594, Shakespeare became an important member of Lord Chamberlain's company of players. This group had the best actors and the best theater, the Globe. For the next 20 years, Shakespeare devoted himself to writing. He died on April 23, 1616, but his works have lived on.

Additional Works by Shakespeare

Love's Labour's Lost (1588–97)
The Comedy of Errors (1589–94)
The Taming of the Shrew (1590–94)
Romeo and Juliet (1594–96)
A Midsummer Night's Dream (1595-96)
Much Ado About Nothing (1598-99)
As You Like It (1598-1600)
Hamlet (1599-1601)
Twelfth Night (1600-02)
Othello (1603-04)
Macbeth (1606-07)
The Tempest (1611)

About the Adapter

Ben Dunn is affectionately called the "Godfather of American Manga." He founded Antarctic Press, one of the largest comic companies in the United States. His works appear in Marvel and Image comics. He is best known for his series *Ninja High School* and *Warrior Nun Areala*.

Glossary

abjure - to reject.

beseech - to beg.

bestow - give a place to stay.

durst - dare.

felicitate - made happy.

hag - a witch.

knave - a young fellow.

nuncle - a form of address from a fool to his master.

opulent - having a large estate or property.

prithee - a way to make a request.

sojourn - a temporary stay.

weed - clothing.

Web Sites

To learn more about William Shakespeare, visit ABDO Publishing Company on the World Wide Web at **www.abdopublishing.com**. Web sites about Shakespeare are featured on our Book Links page. These links are routinely monitored and updated to provide the most current information available.